Pokémon™ X•Y

STORY
Hidenori Kusaka

ART
Satoshi Yamamoto

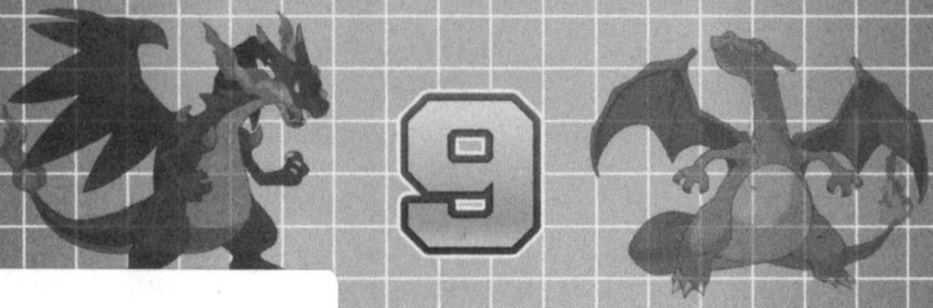

9

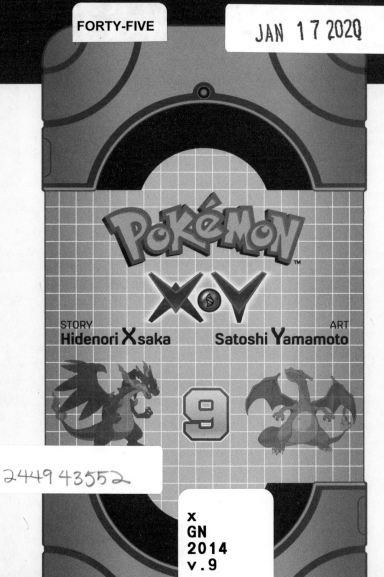

CHARACTERS

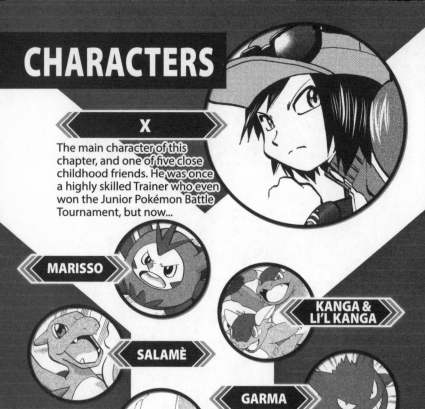

X

The main character of this chapter, and one of five close childhood friends. He was once a highly skilled Trainer who even won the Junior Pokémon Battle Tournament, but now...

MARISSO

KANGA & LI'L KANGA

SALAMÈ

GARMA

ÉLEC

OUR STORY THUS FAR...

In Vaniville Town in the Kalos region, X is a Pokémon Trainer child prodigy. But then he falls into a depression. A sudden attack by the Legendary Pokémon Xerneas and Yveltal, controlled by Team Flare, forces X out into the world again. Now he and his closest childhood friends—Y, Trevor, Tierno and Shauna—are on the run. Then X obtains a ring that Mega Evolves Pokémon, and Team Flare wants to steal it. Turns out Team Flare has a nefarious plan to fire an ancient artifact called the Ultimate Weapon and destroy the Kalos region. After Xerneas allies itself with Y and Yveltal allies itself with Team Flare's Malva, the battle is at a standstill. How will X and his friends increase their power to have a chance of winning the next fight...?!

MEET THE

Y

X's best friend, a Sky Trainer trainee. Her full name is Yvonne Gabena.

TREVOR

One of the five friends. A quiet boy who hopes to become a fine Pokémon Researcher one day.

SHAUNA

One of the five friends. Her dream is to become a Furfrou Groomer. She is quick to speak her mind.

TIERNO

One of the five friends. A big boy with an even bigger heart. He is currently training to become a dancer.

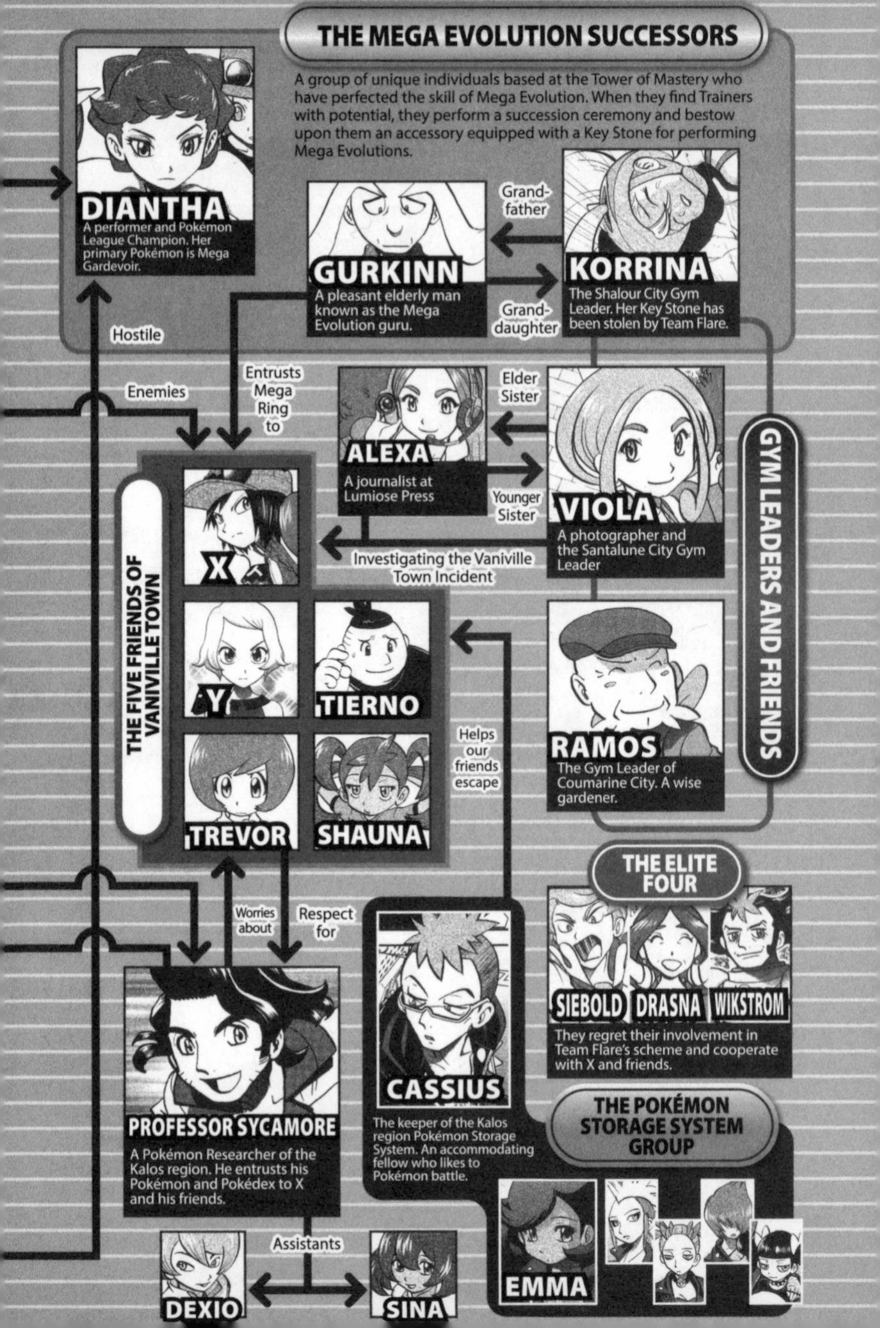
THE MEGA EVOLUTION SUCCESSORS
A group of unique individuals based at the Tower of Mastery who have perfected the skill of Mega Evolution. When they find Trainers with potential, they perform a succession ceremony and bestow upon them an accessory equipped with a Key Stone for performing Mega Evolutions.
DIANTHA
A performer and Pokémon League Champion. Her primary Pokémon is Mega Gardevoir.
GURKINN
A pleasant elderly man known as the Mega Evolution guru.
Grand-father
KORRINA
The Shalour City Gym Leader. Her Key Stone has been stolen by Team Flare.
Grand-daughter
Hostile
Entrusts Mega Ring to
Enemies
ALEXA
A journalist at Lumiose Press
Elder Sister
Younger Sister
VIOLA
A photographer and the Santalune City Gym Leader
Investigating the Vaniville Town Incident
GYM LEADERS AND FRIENDS
THE FIVE FRIENDS OF VANIVILLE TOWN
X
Y
TIERNO
TREVOR
SHAUNA
RAMOS
The Gym Leader of Coumarine City. A wise gardener.
Helps our friends escape
THE ELITE FOUR
SIEBOLD
DRASNA
WIKSTROM
They regret their involvement in Team Flare's scheme and cooperate with X and friends.
Worries about
Respect for
PROFESSOR SYCAMORE
A Pokémon Researcher of the Kalos region. He entrusts his Pokémon and Pokédex to X and his friends.
CASSIUS
The keeper of the Kalos region Pokémon Storage System. An accommodating fellow who likes to Pokémon battle.
THE POKÉMON STORAGE SYSTEM GROUP
EMMA
Assistants
DEXIO
SINA

CHARACTER CORRELATION CHART

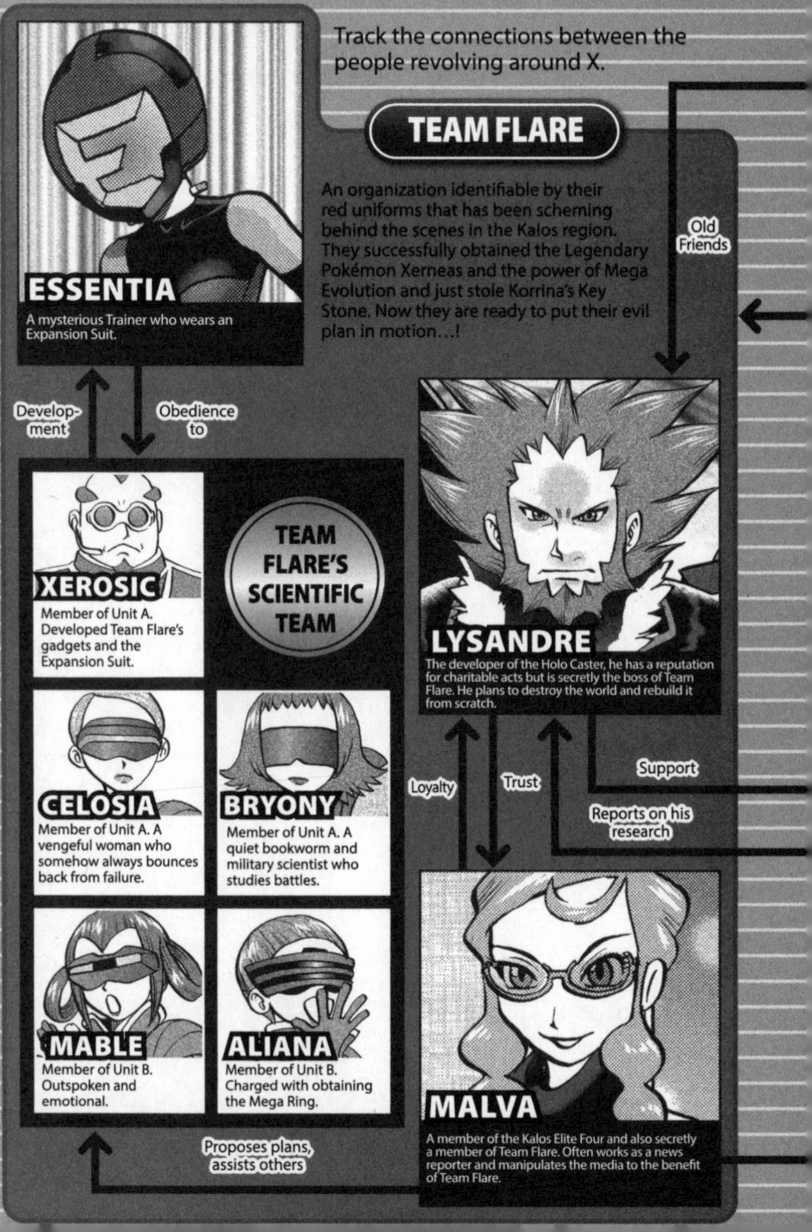

Track the connections between the people revolving around X.
TEAM FLARE
An organization identifiable by their red uniforms that has been scheming behind the scenes in the Kalos region. They successfully obtained the Legendary Pokémon Xerneas and the power of Mega Evolution and just stole Korrina's Key Stone. Now they are ready to put their evil plan in motion…!
Old Friends
ESSENTIA
A mysterious Trainer who wears an Expansion Suit.
Development
Obedience to
TEAM FLARE'S SCIENTIFIC TEAM
XEROSIC
Member of Unit A. Developed Team Flare's gadgets and the Expansion Suit.
CELOSIA
Member of Unit A. A vengeful woman who somehow always bounces back from failure.
BRYONY
Member of Unit A. A quiet bookworm and military scientist who studies battles.
MABLE
Member of Unit B. Outspoken and emotional.
ALIANA
Member of Unit B. Charged with obtaining the Mega Ring.
LYSANDRE
The developer of the Holo Caster, he has a reputation for charitable acts but is secretly the boss of Team Flare. He plans to destroy the world and rebuild it from scratch.
Loyalty
Trust
Support
Reports on his research
MALVA
A member of the Kalos Elite Four and also secretly a member of Team Flare. Often works as a news reporter and manipulates the media to the benefit of Team Flare.
Proposes plans, assists others

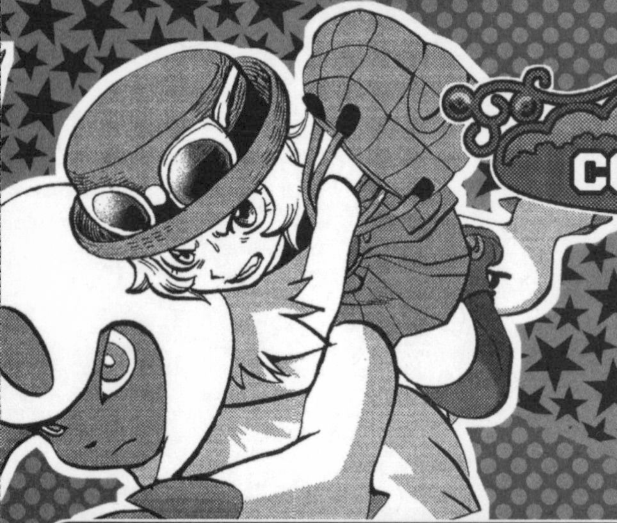

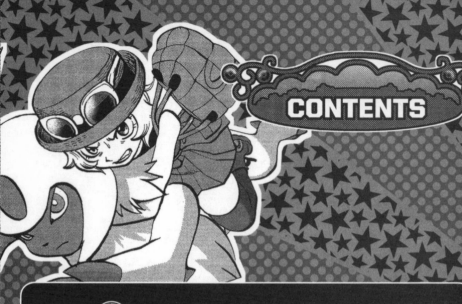

CONTENTS

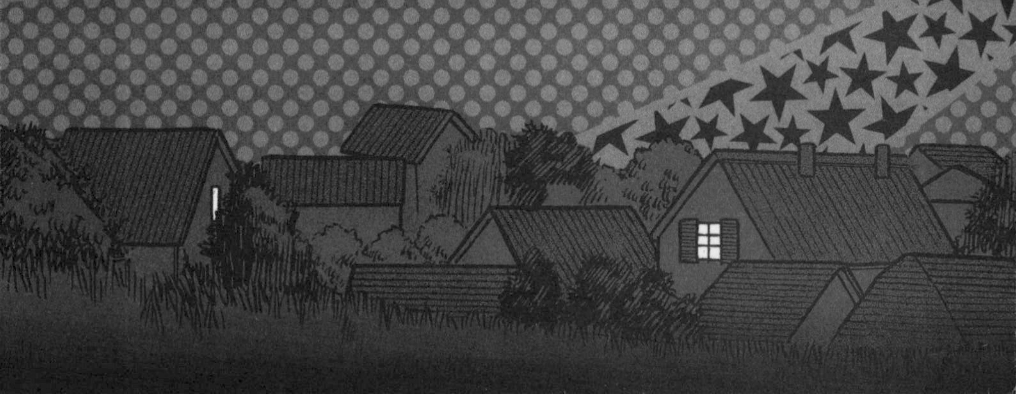

Adventure 28 Scizor Defends

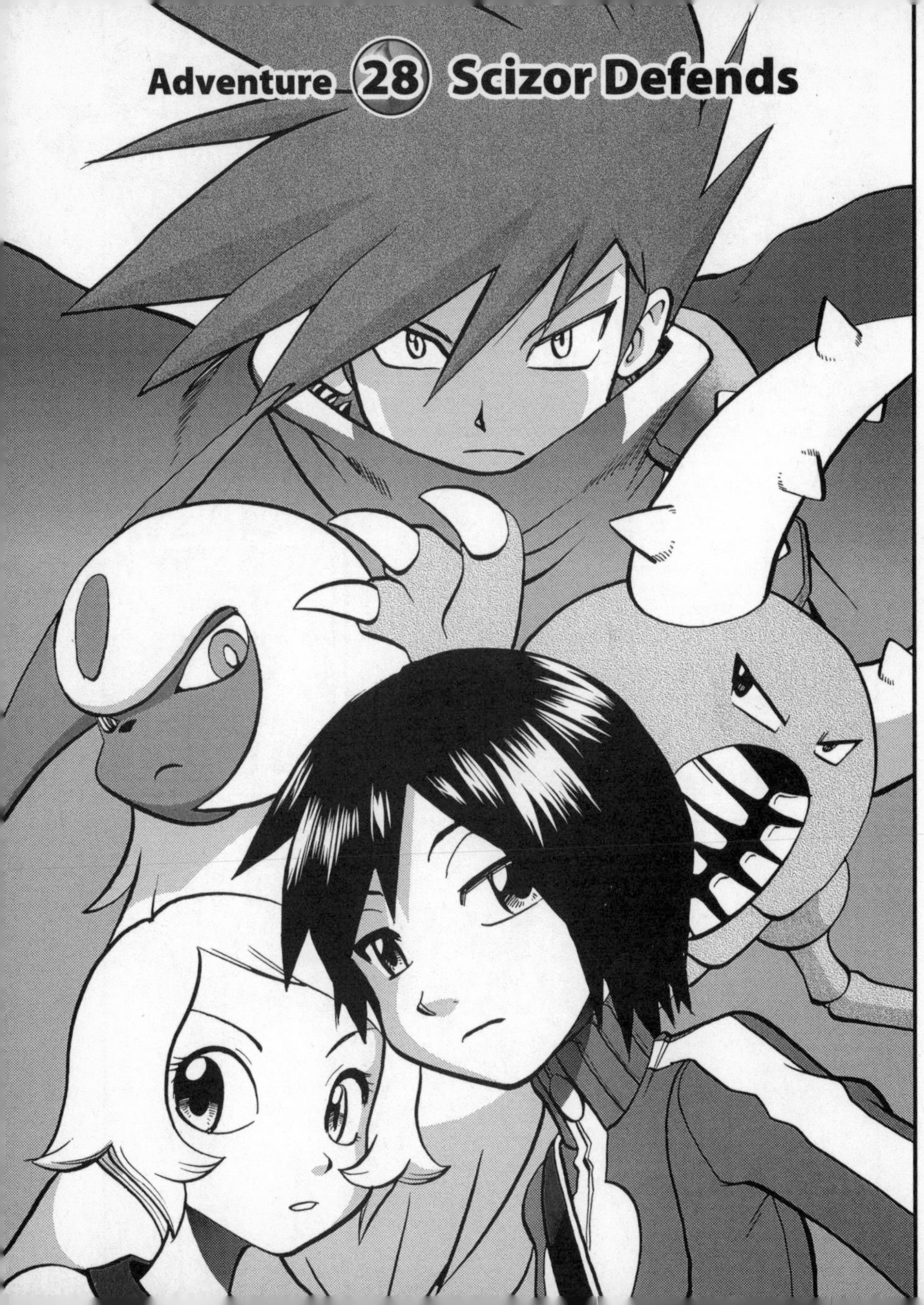

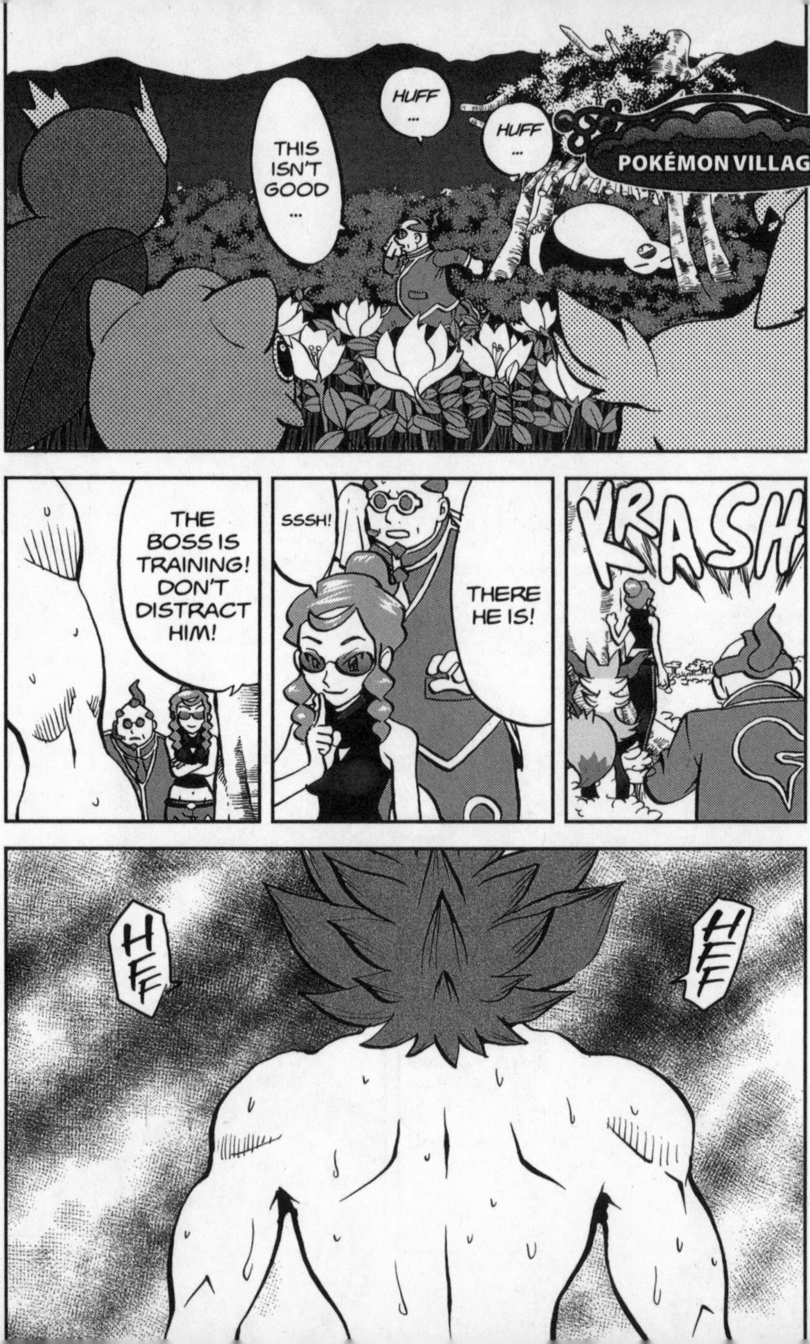
POKÉMON VILLAGE
HUFF ...
HUFF ...
THIS ISN'T GOOD ...
KRASH
THERE HE IS!
SSSH!
THE BOSS IS TRAINING! DON'T DISTRACT HIM!
HEFF
HEFF

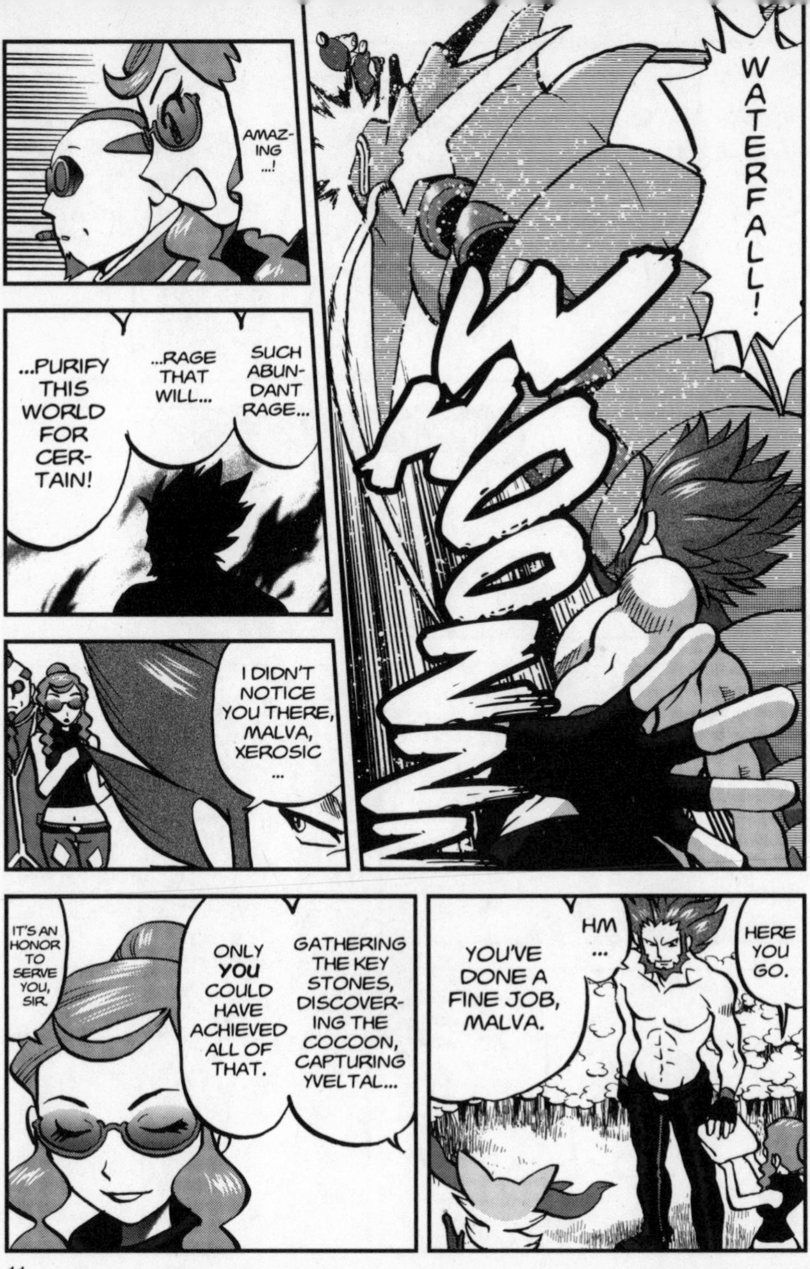
WATERFALL!
AMAZ-ING ...!
SUCH ABUN-DANT RAGE...
...RAGE THAT WILL...
...PURIFY THIS WORLD FOR CER-TAIN!
I DIDN'T NOTICE YOU THERE, MALVA, XEROSIC ...
HERE YOU GO.
HM ...
YOU'VE DONE A FINE JOB, MALVA.
GATHERING THE KEY STONES, DISCOVER-ING THE COCOON, CAPTURING YVELTAL...
ONLY **YOU** COULD HAVE ACHIEVED ALL OF THAT.
IT'S AN HONOR TO SERVE YOU, SIR.

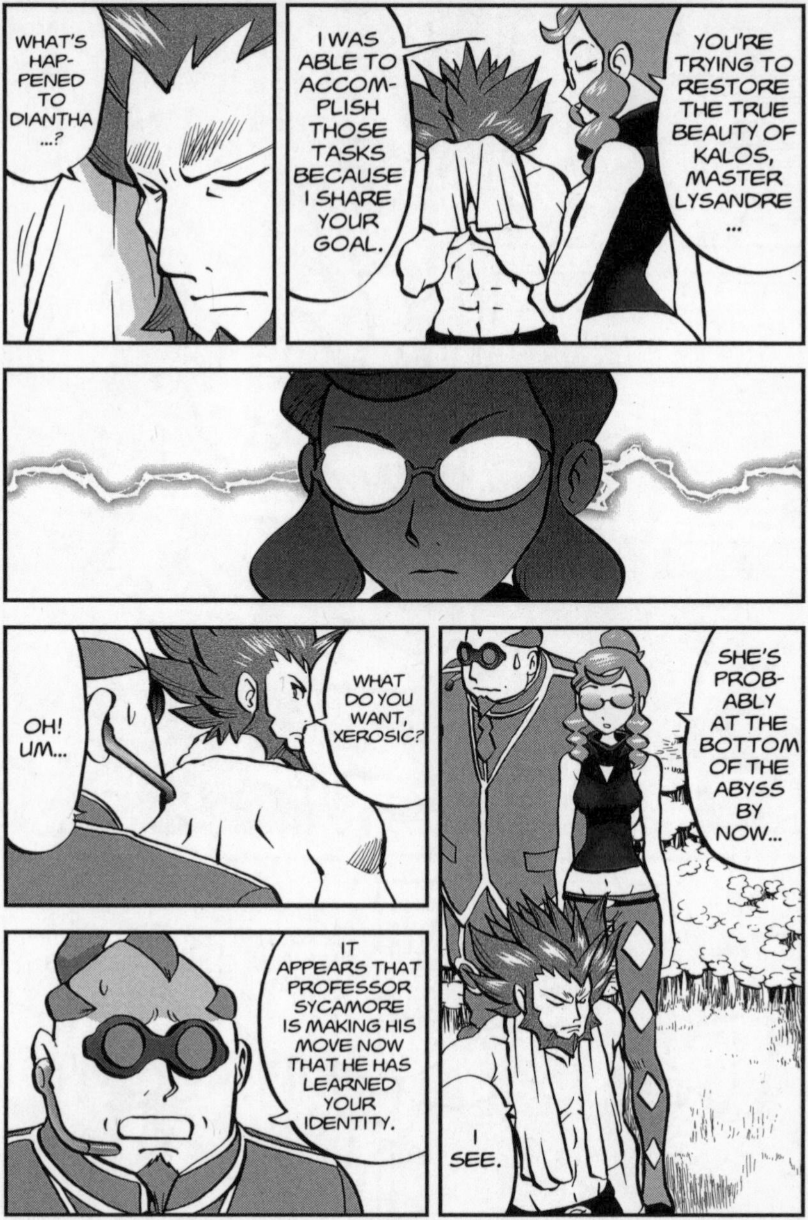
YOU'RE TRYING TO RESTORE THE TRUE BEAUTY OF KALOS, MASTER LYSANDRE ...
I WAS ABLE TO ACCOMPLISH THOSE TASKS BECAUSE I SHARE YOUR GOAL.
WHAT'S HAPPENED TO DIANTHA ...?
SHE'S PROBABLY AT THE BOTTOM OF THE ABYSS BY NOW...
I SEE.
WHAT DO YOU WANT, XEROSIC?
OH! UM...
IT APPEARS THAT PROFESSOR SYCAMORE IS MAKING HIS MOVE NOW THAT HE HAS LEARNED YOUR IDENTITY.

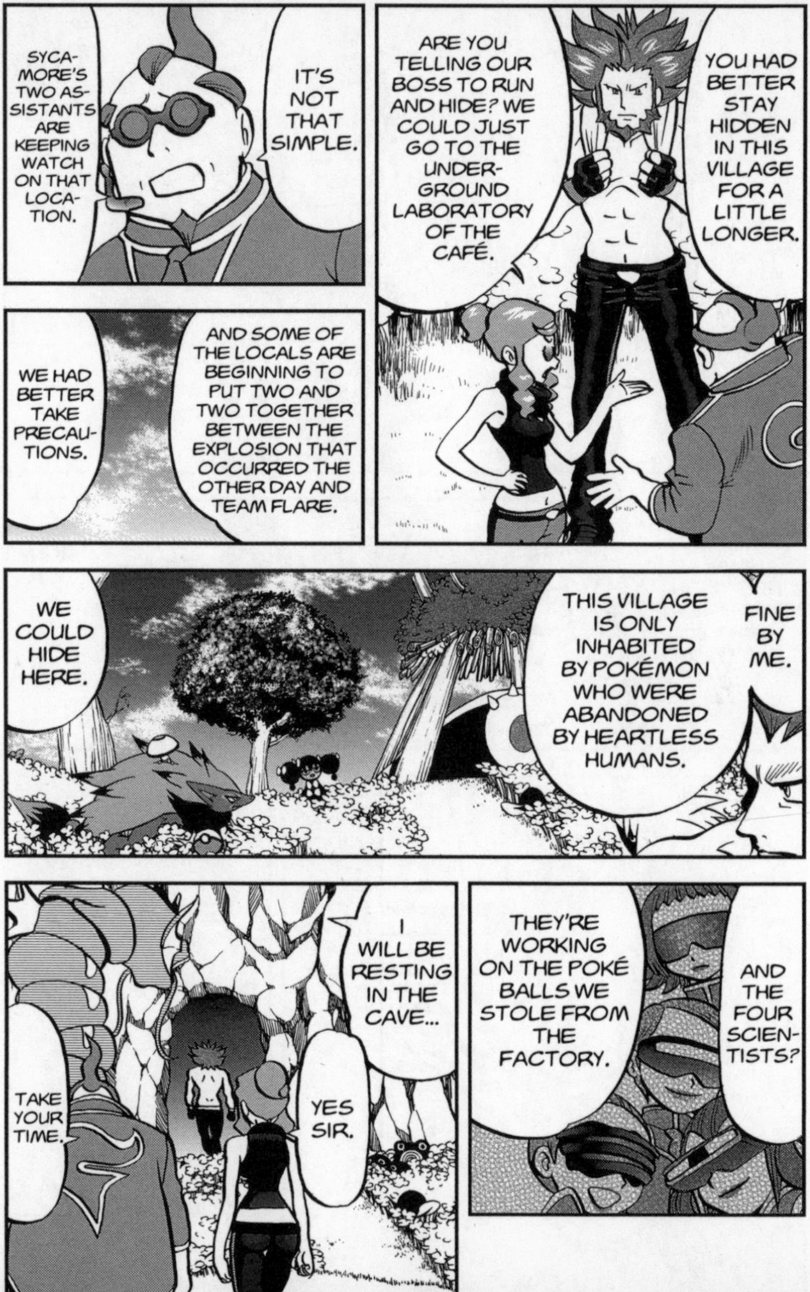
YOU HAD BETTER STAY HIDDEN IN THIS VILLAGE FOR A LITTLE LONGER.
ARE YOU TELLING OUR BOSS TO RUN AND HIDE? WE COULD JUST GO TO THE UNDERGROUND LABORATORY OF THE CAFÉ.
IT'S NOT THAT SIMPLE.
SYCAMORE'S TWO ASSISTANTS ARE KEEPING WATCH ON THAT LOCATION.
AND SOME OF THE LOCALS ARE BEGINNING TO PUT TWO AND TWO TOGETHER BETWEEN THE EXPLOSION THAT OCCURRED THE OTHER DAY AND TEAM FLARE.
WE HAD BETTER TAKE PRECAUTIONS.
FINE BY ME.
THIS VILLAGE IS ONLY INHABITED BY POKÉMON WHO WERE ABANDONED BY HEARTLESS HUMANS.
WE COULD HIDE HERE.
AND THE FOUR SCIENTISTS?
THEY'RE WORKING ON THE POKÉ BALLS WE STOLE FROM THE FACTORY.
I WILL BE RESTING IN THE CAVE...
YES SIR.
TAKE YOUR TIME.

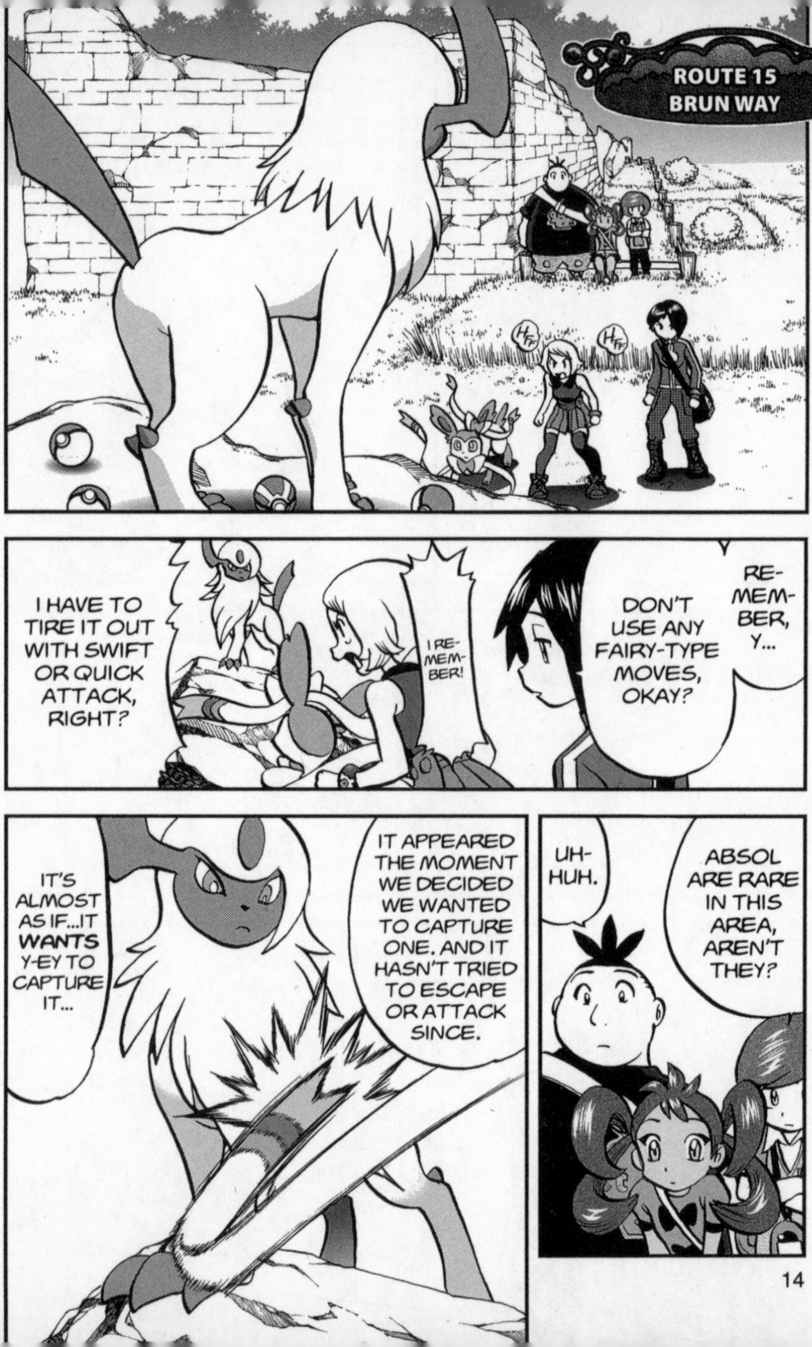
ROUTE 15
BRUN WAY
HFF
HFF
RE-MEM-BER, Y...
DON'T USE ANY FAIRY-TYPE MOVES, OKAY?
I RE-MEM-BER!
I HAVE TO TIRE IT OUT WITH SWIFT OR QUICK ATTACK, RIGHT?
ABSOL ARE RARE IN THIS AREA, AREN'T THEY?
UH-HUH.
IT APPEARED THE MOMENT WE DECIDED WE WANTED TO CAPTURE ONE. AND IT HASN'T TRIED TO ESCAPE OR ATTACK SINCE.
IT'S ALMOST AS IF...IT **WANTS** Y-EY TO CAPTURE IT...

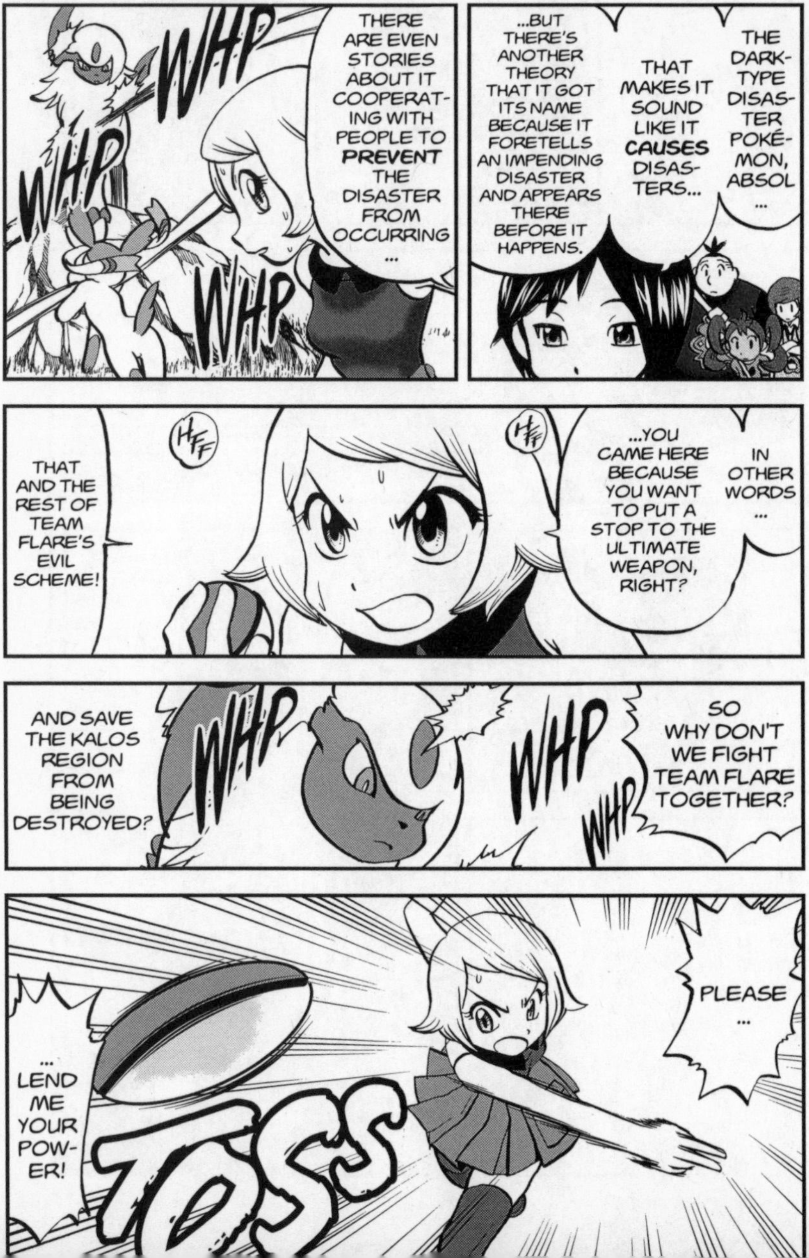
THE DARK-TYPE DISASTER POKÉMON, ABSOL...
THAT MAKES IT SOUND LIKE IT **CAUSES** DISASTERS...
...BUT THERE'S ANOTHER THEORY THAT IT GOT ITS NAME BECAUSE IT FORETELLS AN IMPENDING DISASTER AND APPEARS THERE BEFORE IT HAPPENS.
THERE ARE EVEN STORIES ABOUT IT COOPERATING WITH PEOPLE TO **PREVENT** THE DISASTER FROM OCCURRING...
WHP
WHP
WHP
IN OTHER WORDS...
...YOU CAME HERE BECAUSE YOU WANT TO PUT A STOP TO THE ULTIMATE WEAPON, RIGHT?
HFF
HFF
THAT AND THE REST OF TEAM FLARE'S EVIL SCHEME!
SO WHY DON'T WE FIGHT TEAM FLARE TOGETHER?
WHP
WHP
WHP
AND SAVE THE KALOS REGION FROM BEING DESTROYED?
PLEASE...
...LEND ME YOUR POWER!
TOSS

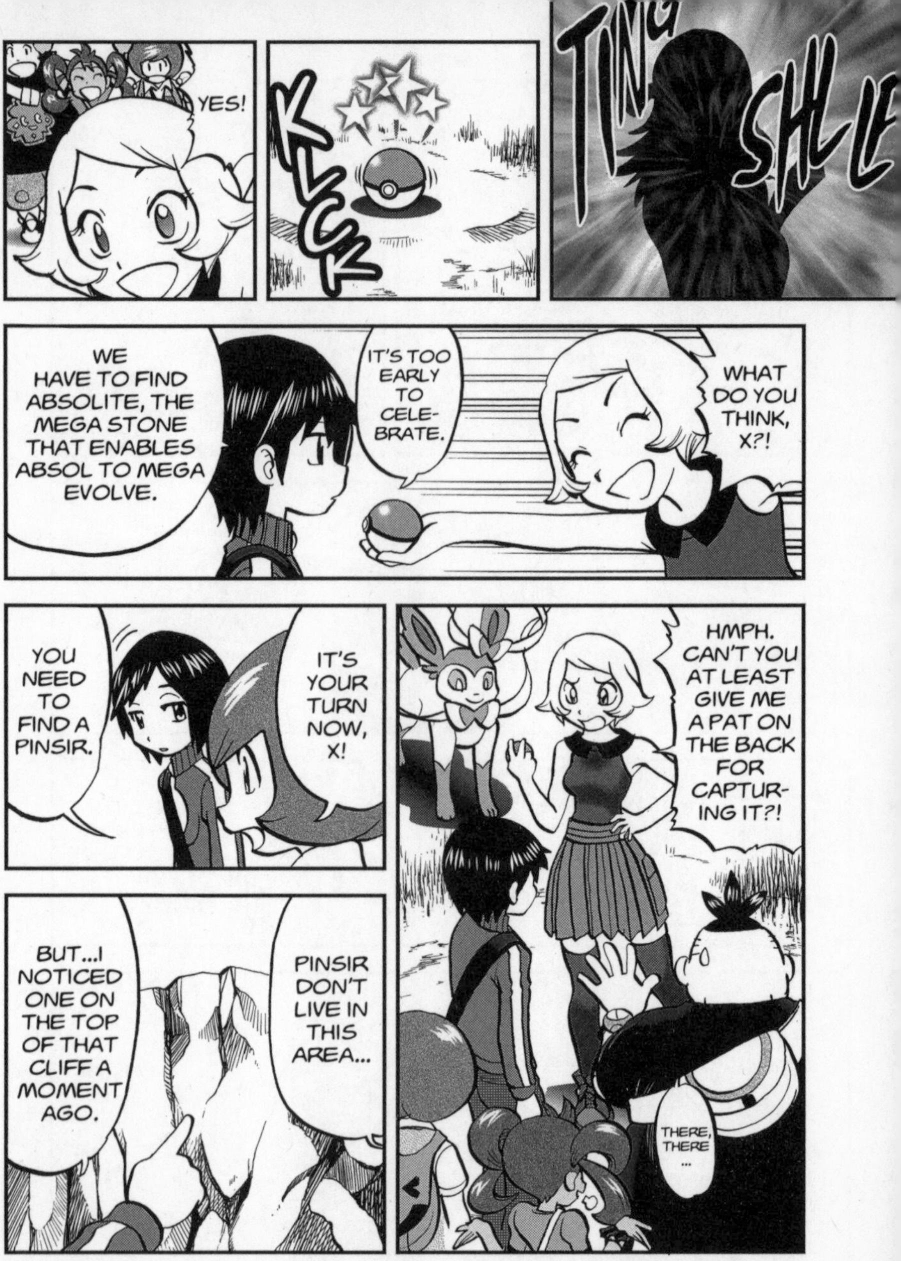

TING
SHLE
KLICK
YES!
WHAT DO YOU THINK, X?!
IT'S TOO EARLY TO CELEBRATE.
WE HAVE TO FIND ABSOLITE, THE MEGA STONE THAT ENABLES ABSOL TO MEGA EVOLVE.
HMPH. CAN'T YOU AT LEAST GIVE ME A PAT ON THE BACK FOR CAPTURING IT?!
THERE, THERE ...
IT'S YOUR TURN NOW, X!
YOU NEED TO FIND A PINSIR.
PINSIR DON'T LIVE IN THIS AREA...
BUT...I NOTICED ONE ON THE TOP OF THAT CLIFF A MOMENT AGO.

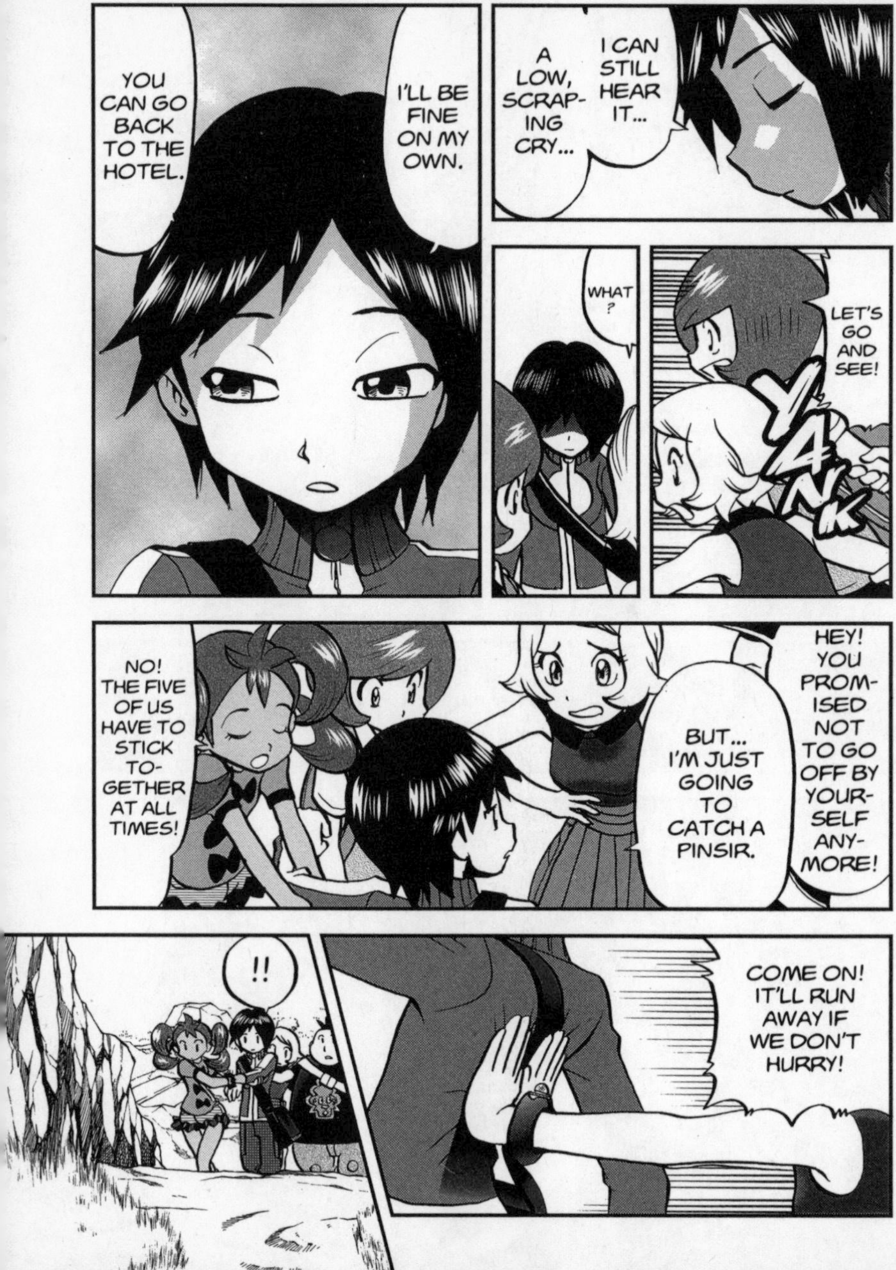
I CAN STILL HEAR IT...
A LOW, SCRAPING CRY...
LET'S GO AND SEE!
YANK
WHAT?
I'LL BE FINE ON MY OWN.
YOU CAN GO BACK TO THE HOTEL.
HEY! YOU PROMISED NOT TO GO OFF BY YOURSELF ANYMORE!
BUT... I'M JUST GOING TO CATCH A PINSIR.
NO! THE FIVE OF US HAVE TO STICK TOGETHER AT ALL TIMES!
COME ON! IT'LL RUN AWAY IF WE DON'T HURRY!
!!

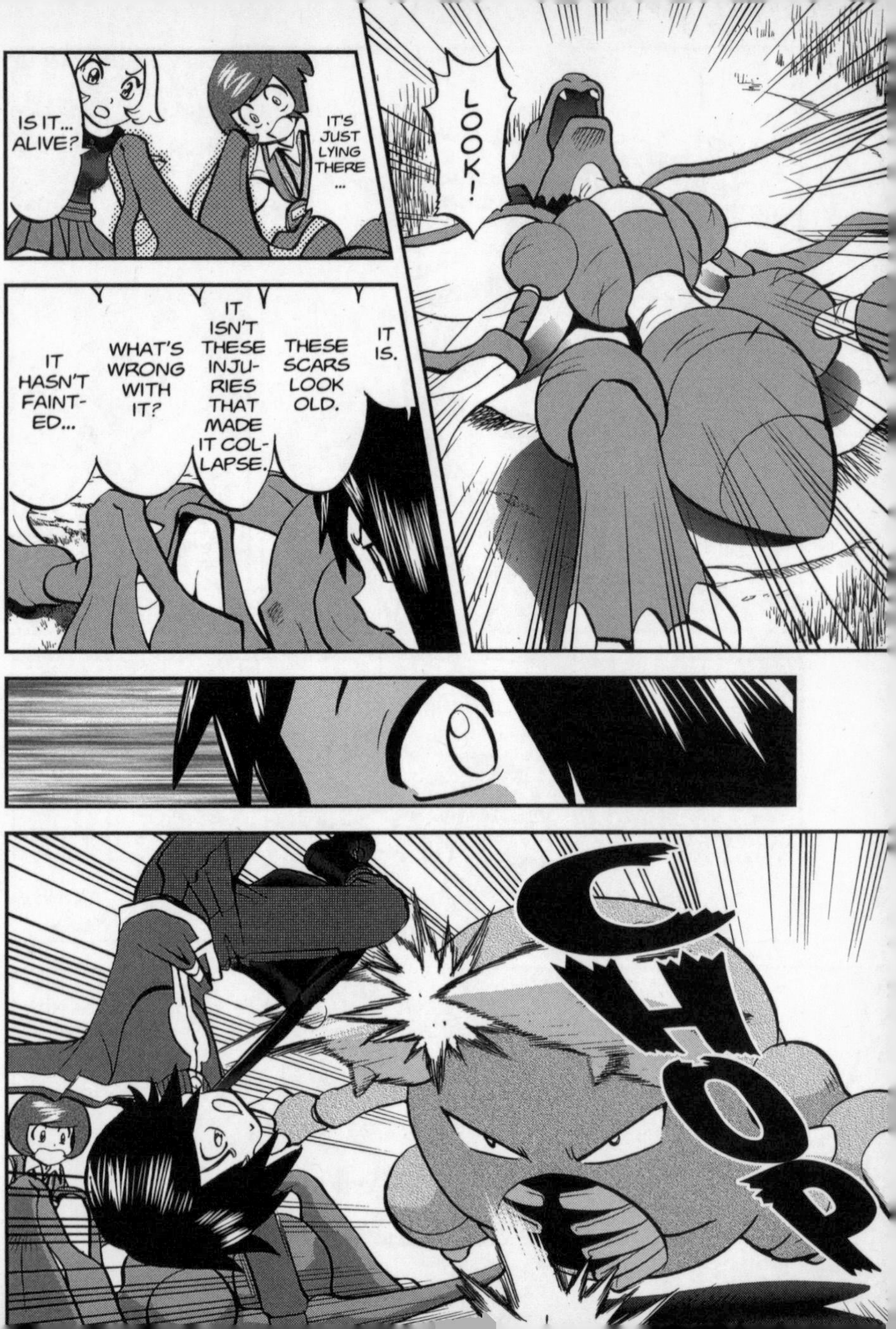
LOOK!
IT'S JUST LYING THERE...
IS IT... ALIVE?
IT IS.
THESE SCARS LOOK OLD.
IT ISN'T THESE INJURIES THAT MADE IT COLLAPSE.
WHAT'S WRONG WITH IT?
IT HASN'T FAINTED...
CHOP

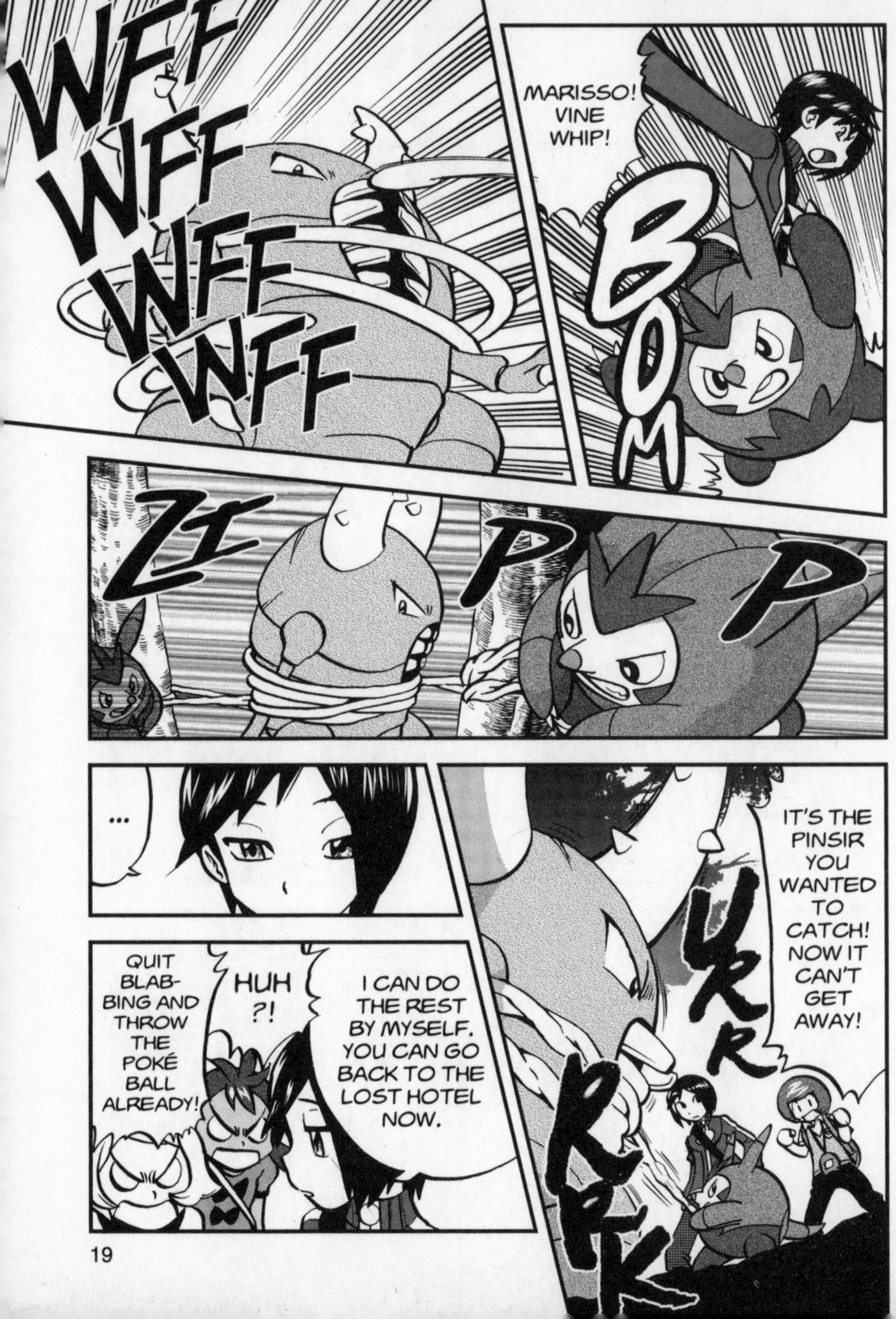
MARISSO! VINE WHIP!
BOOM
WFF WFF WFF WFF
ZIPPP
IT'S THE PINSIR YOU WANTED TO CATCH! NOW IT CAN'T GET AWAY!
URRKKK
...
I CAN DO THE REST BY MYSELF. YOU CAN GO BACK TO THE LOST HOTEL NOW.
HUH ?!
QUIT BLAB-BING AND THROW THE POKÉ BALL ALREADY!

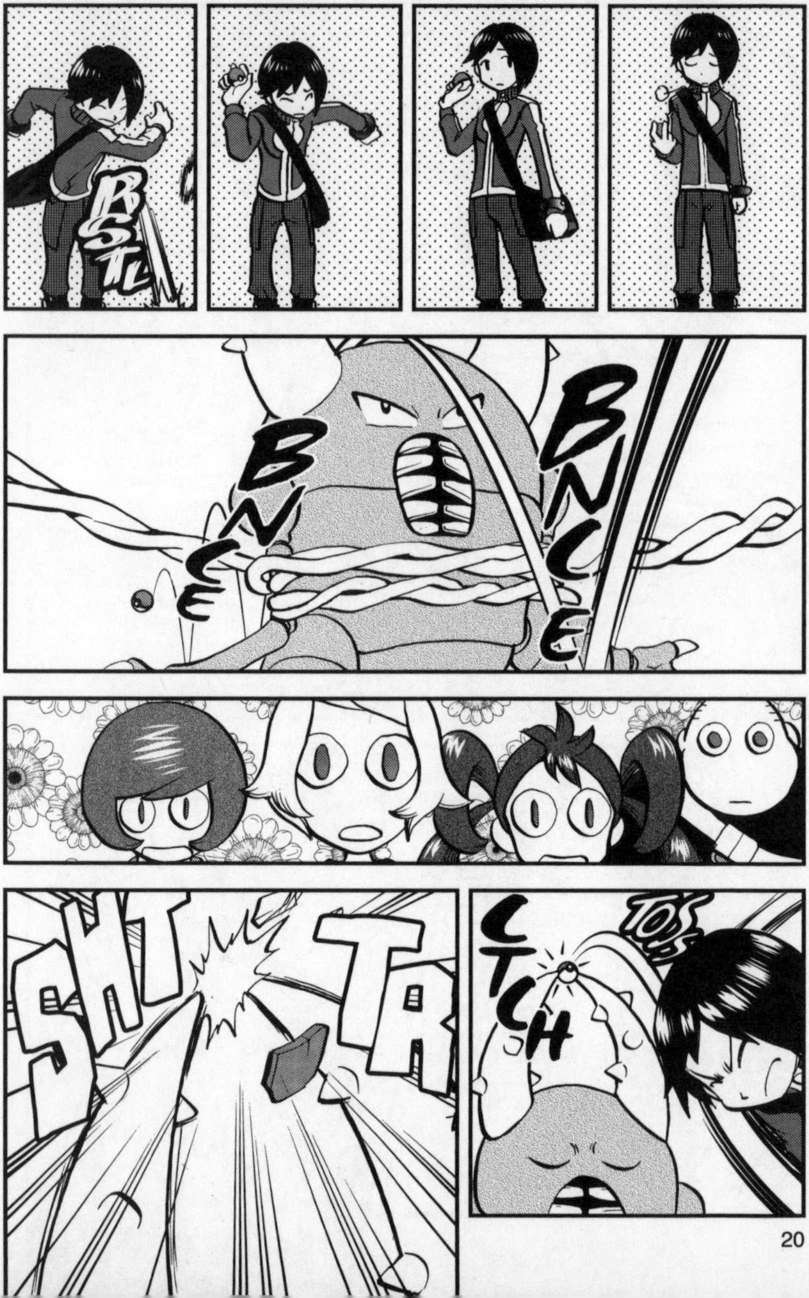
RSTL
BNCE
BNCE
TOS
CTCH
SHT
TR

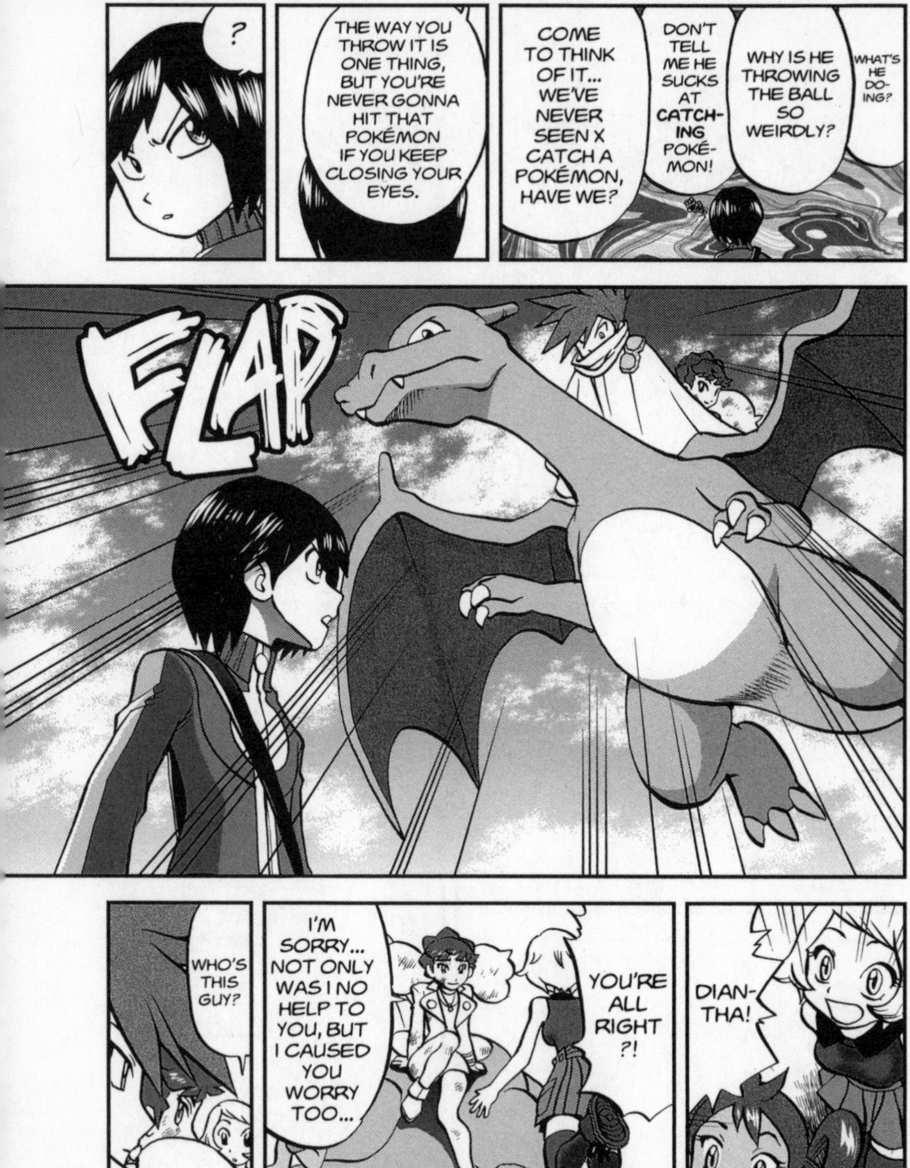
WHAT'S HE DO-ING?
WHY IS HE THROWING THE BALL SO WEIRDLY?
DON'T TELL ME HE SUCKS AT **CATCHING** POKÉMON!
COME TO THINK OF IT... WE'VE NEVER SEEN X CATCH A POKÉMON, HAVE WE?
THE WAY YOU THROW IT IS ONE THING, BUT YOU'RE NEVER GONNA HIT THAT POKÉMON IF YOU KEEP CLOSING YOUR EYES.
?
FLAP
DIAN-THA!
YOU'RE ALL RIGHT ?!
I'M SORRY... NOT ONLY WAS I NO HELP TO YOU, BUT I CAUSED YOU WORRY TOO...
WHO'S THIS GUY?

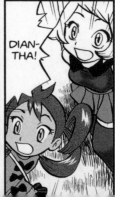

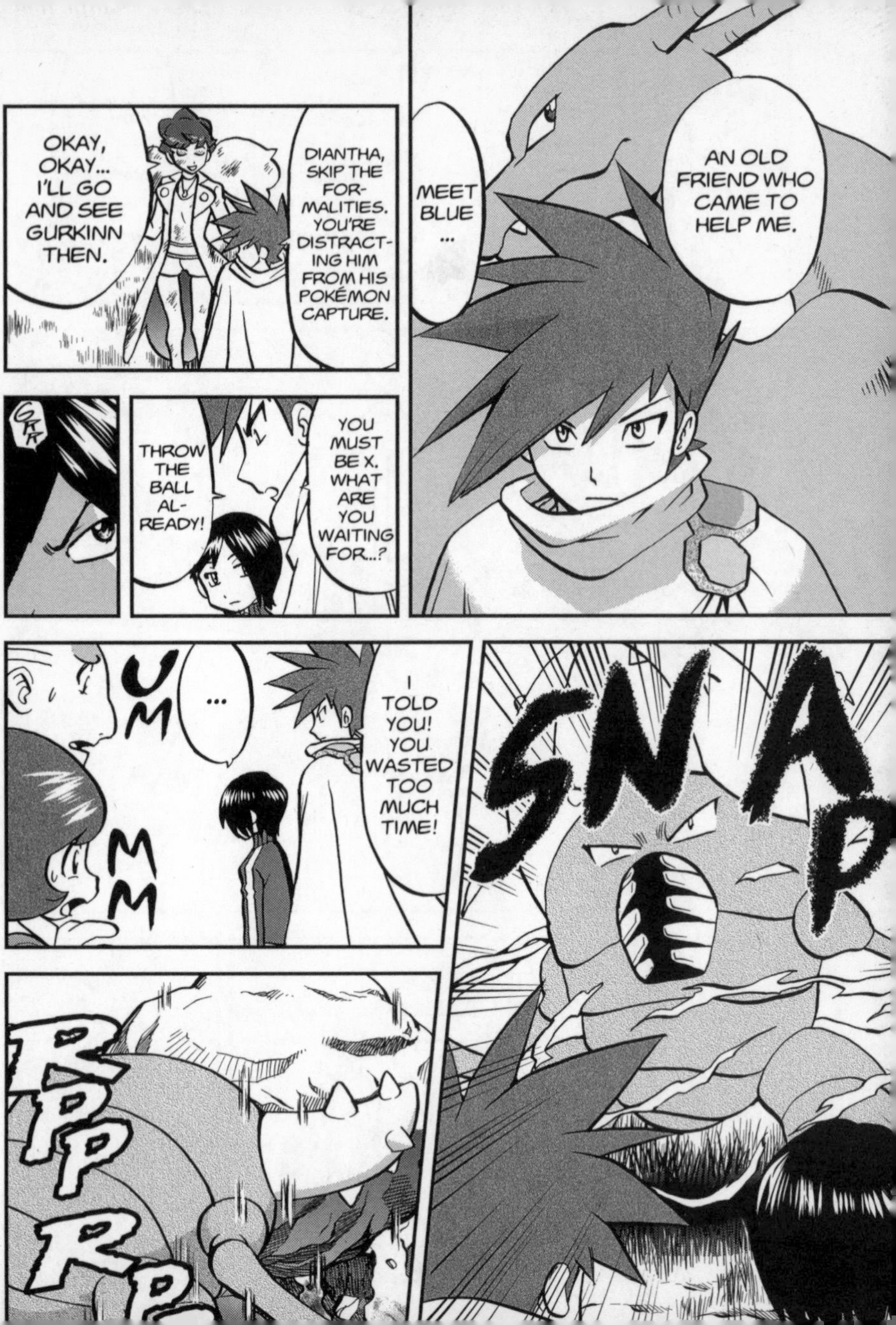

MEET BLUE ...
AN OLD FRIEND WHO CAME TO HELP ME.
DIANTHA, SKIP THE FOR-MALITIES. YOU'RE DISTRACT-ING HIM FROM HIS POKÉMON CAPTURE.
OKAY, OKAY... I'LL GO AND SEE GURKINN THEN.
YOU MUST BE X. WHAT ARE YOU WAITING FOR...?
THROW THE BALL AL-READY!
GRR
SNAP
I TOLD YOU! YOU WASTED TOO MUCH TIME!
...
UMM MM
RPP RRP

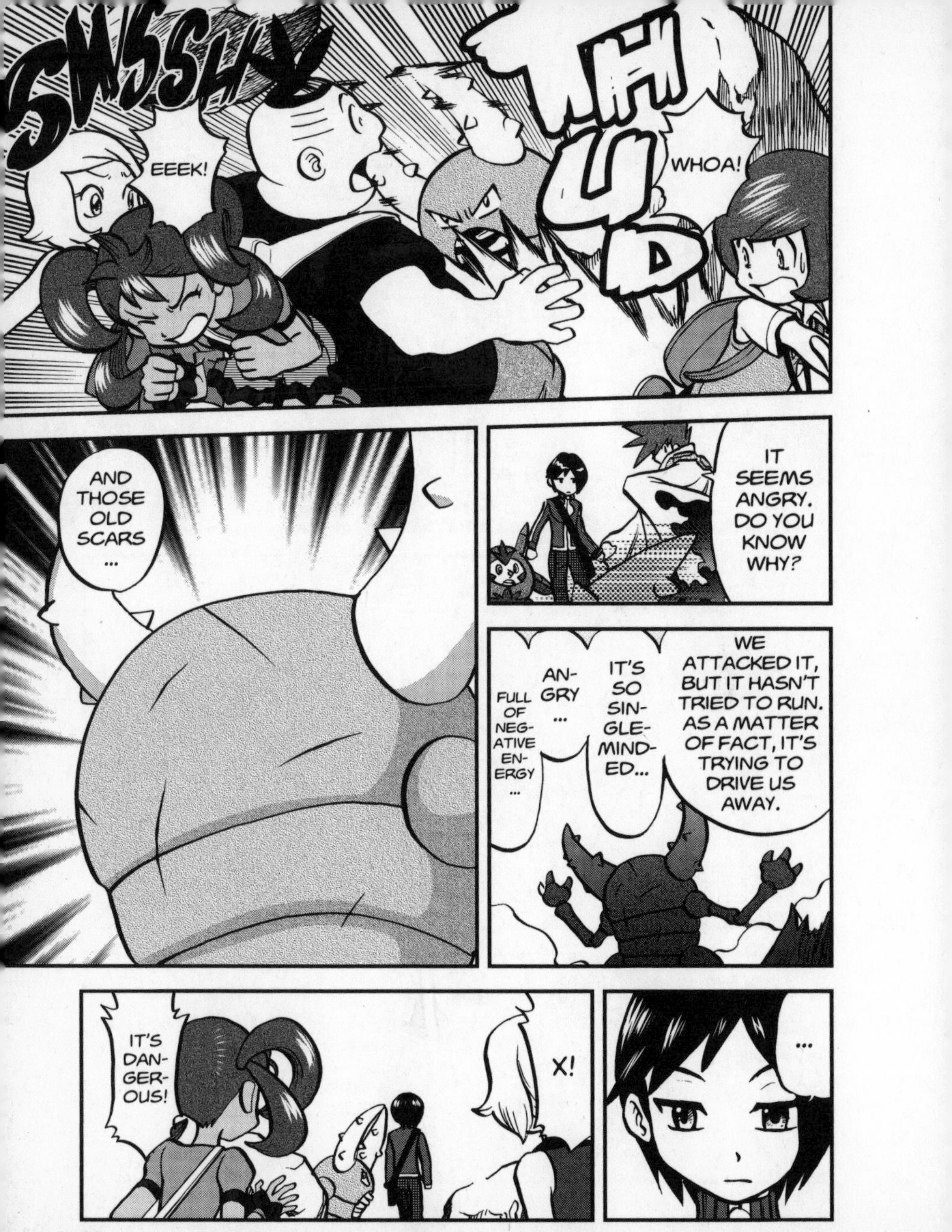
WHOA!
WHUD
EEEK!
SWSSH
IT SEEMS ANGRY. DO YOU KNOW WHY?
WE ATTACKED IT, BUT IT HASN'T TRIED TO RUN. AS A MATTER OF FACT, IT'S TRYING TO DRIVE US AWAY.
IT'S SO SINGLE-MINDED...
ANGRY...
FULL OF NEGATIVE ENERGY...
AND THOSE OLD SCARS...
...
X!
IT'S DANGEROUS!

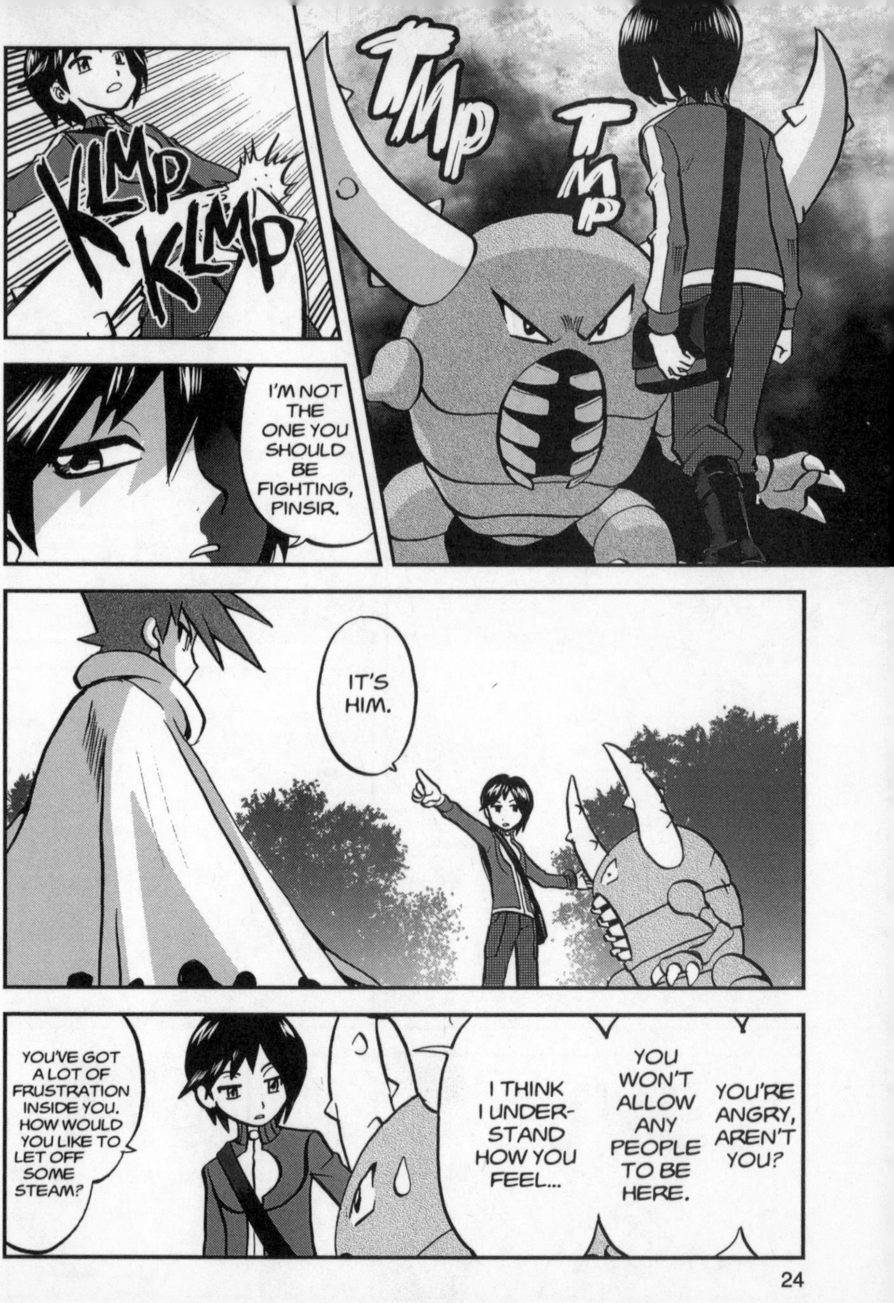
TMP
TMP
KLMP KLMP
I'M NOT THE ONE YOU SHOULD BE FIGHTING, PINSIR.
IT'S HIM.
YOU'RE ANGRY, AREN'T YOU?
YOU WON'T ALLOW ANY PEOPLE TO BE HERE.
I THINK I UNDER-STAND HOW YOU FEEL...
YOU'VE GOT A LOT OF FRUSTRATION INSIDE YOU. HOW WOULD YOU LIKE TO LET OFF SOME STEAM?

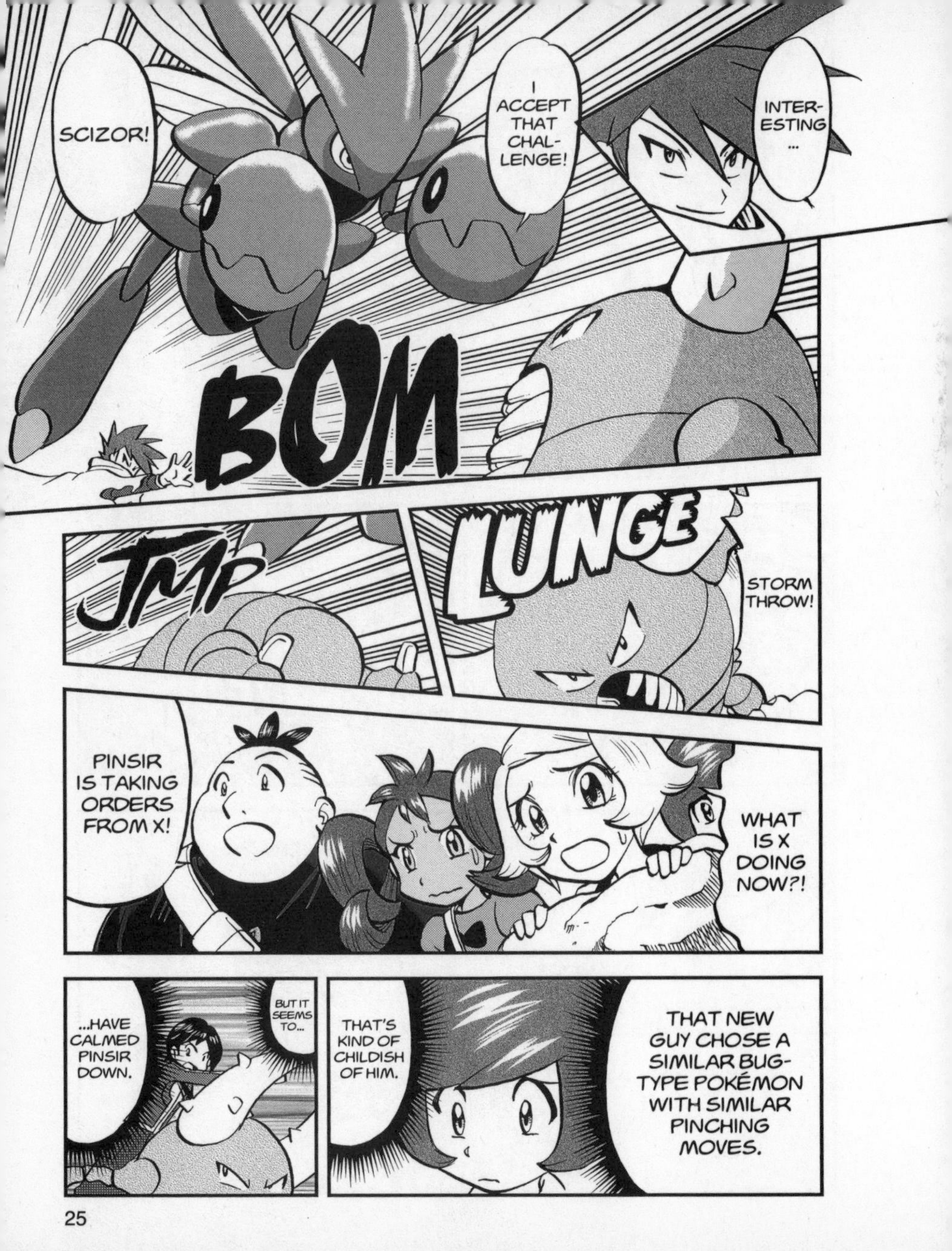
INTERESTING...
I ACCEPT THAT CHALLENGE!
SCIZOR!
BOM
LUNGE
STORM THROW!
JMP
WHAT IS X DOING NOW?!
PINSIR IS TAKING ORDERS FROM X!
THAT NEW GUY CHOSE A SIMILAR BUG-TYPE POKÉMON WITH SIMILAR PINCHING MOVES.
THAT'S KIND OF CHILDISH OF HIM.
BUT IT SEEMS TO...
...HAVE CALMED PINSIR DOWN.

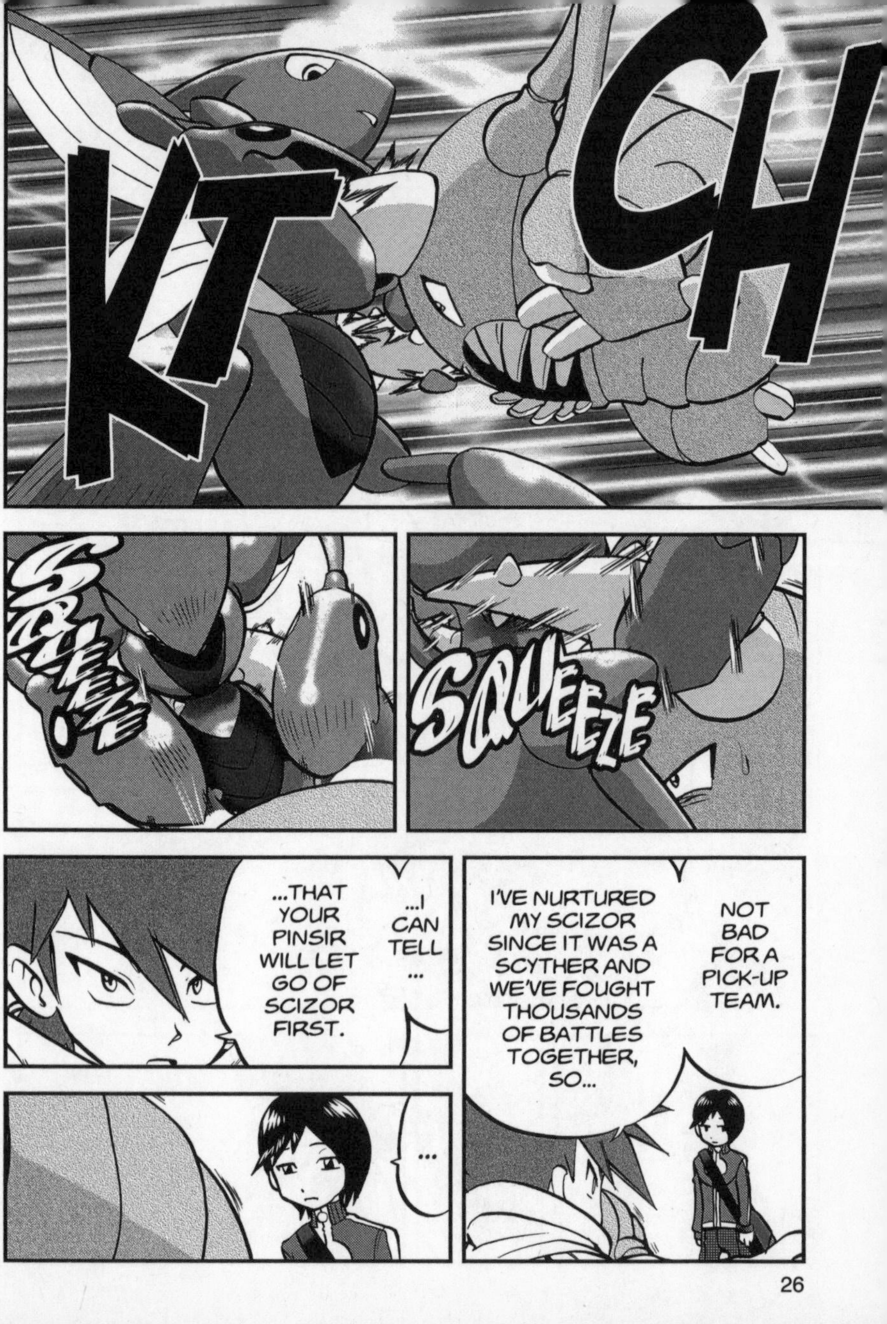
KITCH
SQUEEZE
SQUEEZE
NOT BAD FOR A PICK-UP TEAM.
I'VE NURTURED MY SCIZOR SINCE IT WAS A SCYTHER AND WE'VE FOUGHT THOUSANDS OF BATTLES TOGETHER, SO...
...I CAN TELL...
...THAT YOUR PINSIR WILL LET GO OF SCIZOR FIRST.
...

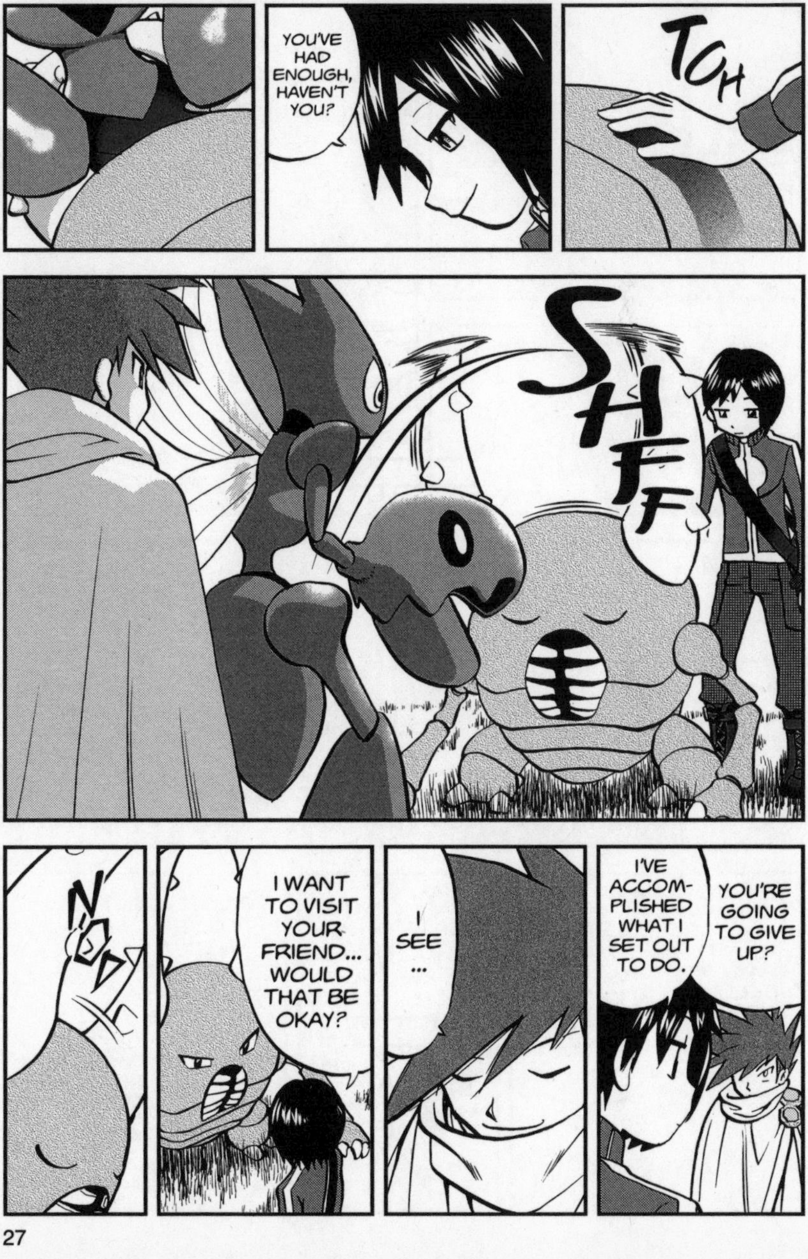
TOH
YOU'VE HAD ENOUGH, HAVEN'T YOU?
SHFF
YOU'RE GOING TO GIVE UP?
I'VE ACCOM-PLISHED WHAT I SET OUT TO DO.
I SEE ...
I WANT TO VISIT YOUR FRIEND... WOULD THAT BE OKAY?
NOD

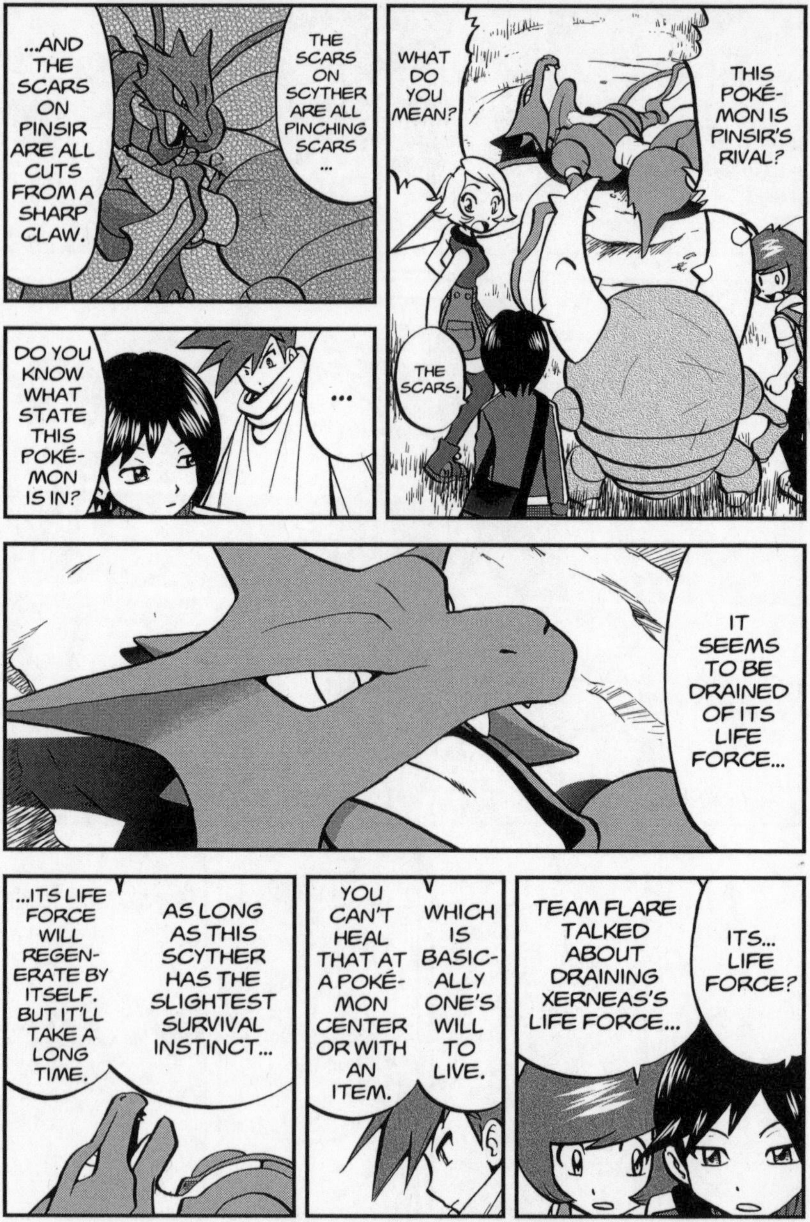
THIS POKÉMON IS PINSIR'S RIVAL?
WHAT DO YOU MEAN?
THE SCARS.
THE SCARS ON SCYTHER ARE ALL PINCHING SCARS ...
...AND THE SCARS ON PINSIR ARE ALL CUTS FROM A SHARP CLAW.
...
DO YOU KNOW WHAT STATE THIS POKÉMON IS IN?
IT SEEMS TO BE DRAINED OF ITS LIFE FORCE...
ITS... LIFE FORCE?
TEAM FLARE TALKED ABOUT DRAINING XERNEAS'S LIFE FORCE...
WHICH IS BASICALLY ONE'S WILL TO LIVE.
YOU CAN'T HEAL THAT AT A POKÉMON CENTER OR WITH AN ITEM.
AS LONG AS THIS SCYTHER HAS THE SLIGHTEST SURVIVAL INSTINCT...
...ITS LIFE FORCE WILL REGENERATE BY ITSELF. BUT IT'LL TAKE A LONG TIME.

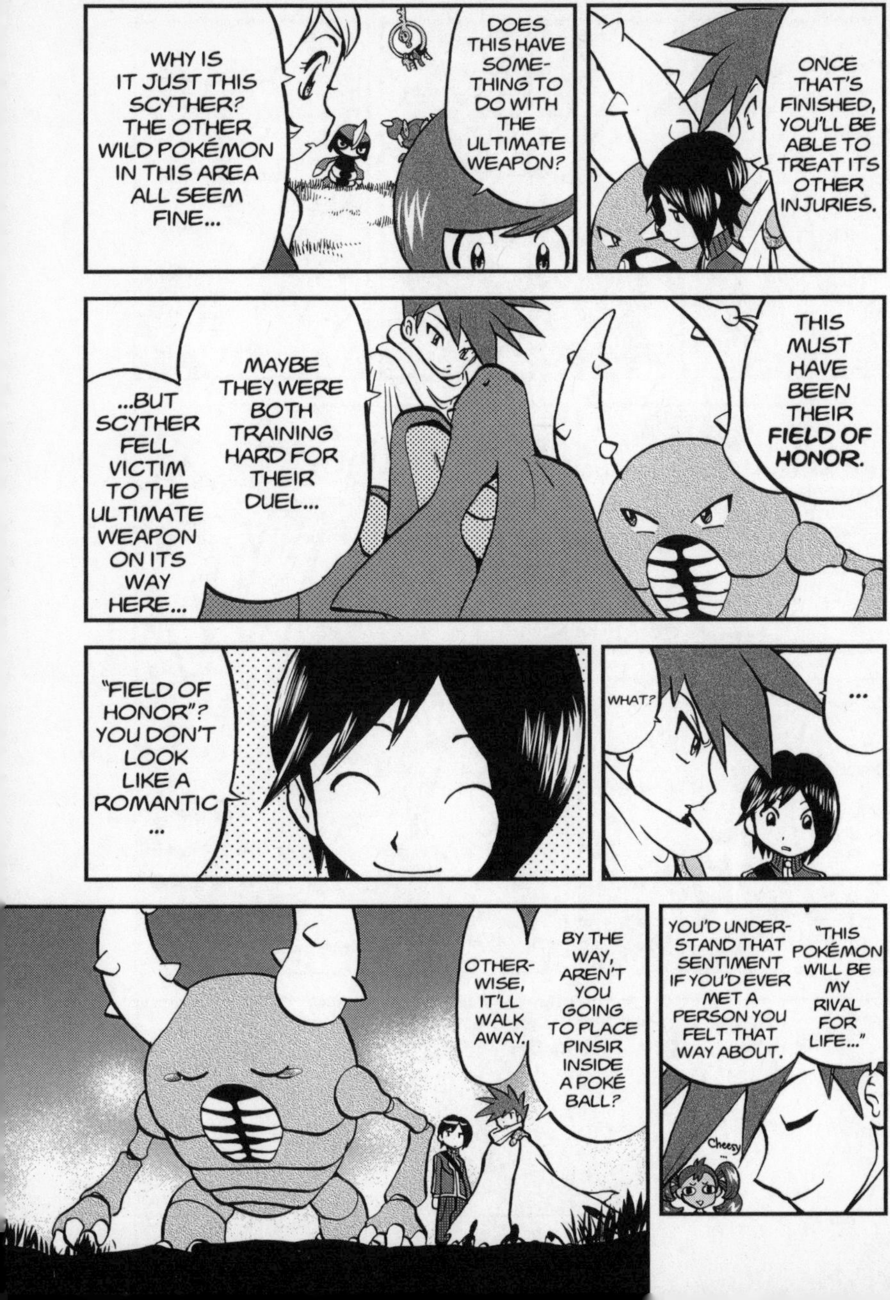
ONCE THAT'S FINISHED, YOU'LL BE ABLE TO TREAT ITS OTHER INJURIES.
DOES THIS HAVE SOMETHING TO DO WITH THE ULTIMATE WEAPON?
WHY IS IT JUST THIS SCYTHER? THE OTHER WILD POKÉMON IN THIS AREA ALL SEEM FINE...
THIS MUST HAVE BEEN THEIR **FIELD OF HONOR.**
MAYBE THEY WERE BOTH TRAINING HARD FOR THEIR DUEL...
...BUT SCYTHER FELL VICTIM TO THE ULTIMATE WEAPON ON ITS WAY HERE...
...
WHAT?
"FIELD OF HONOR"? YOU DON'T LOOK LIKE A ROMANTIC...
"THIS POKÉMON WILL BE MY RIVAL FOR LIFE..."
YOU'D UNDERSTAND THAT SENTIMENT IF YOU'D EVER MET A PERSON YOU FELT THAT WAY ABOUT.
Cheesy...
BY THE WAY, AREN'T YOU GOING TO PLACE PINSIR INSIDE A POKÉ BALL?
OTHERWISE, IT'LL WALK AWAY.

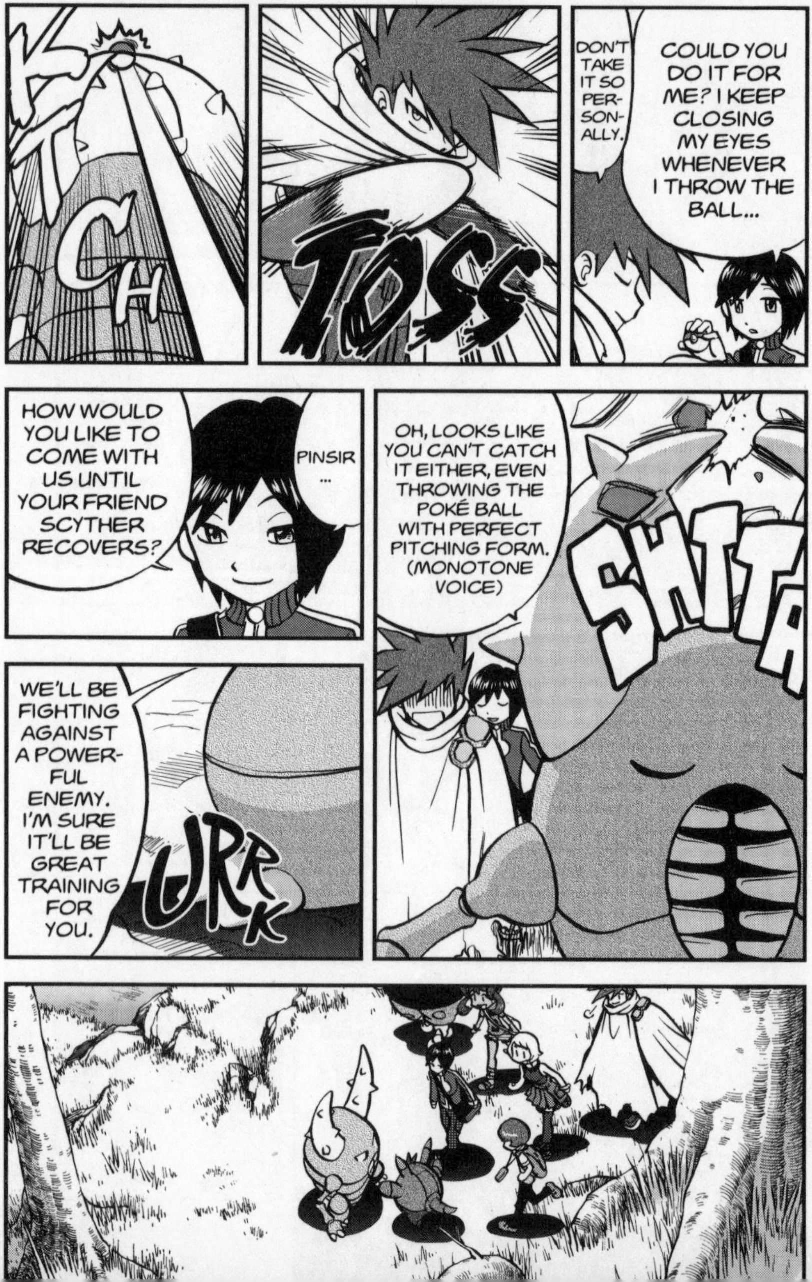
COULD YOU DO IT FOR ME? I KEEP CLOSING MY EYES WHENEVER I THROW THE BALL...
DON'T TAKE IT SO PERSONALLY.
TOSS
KTCH
OH, LOOKS LIKE YOU CAN'T CATCH IT EITHER, EVEN THROWING THE POKÉ BALL WITH PERFECT PITCHING FORM. (MONOTONE VOICE)
SHTTA
PINSIR...
HOW WOULD YOU LIKE TO COME WITH US UNTIL YOUR FRIEND SCYTHER RECOVERS?
WE'LL BE FIGHTING AGAINST A POWERFUL ENEMY. I'M SURE IT'LL BE GREAT TRAINING FOR YOU.
URRRK

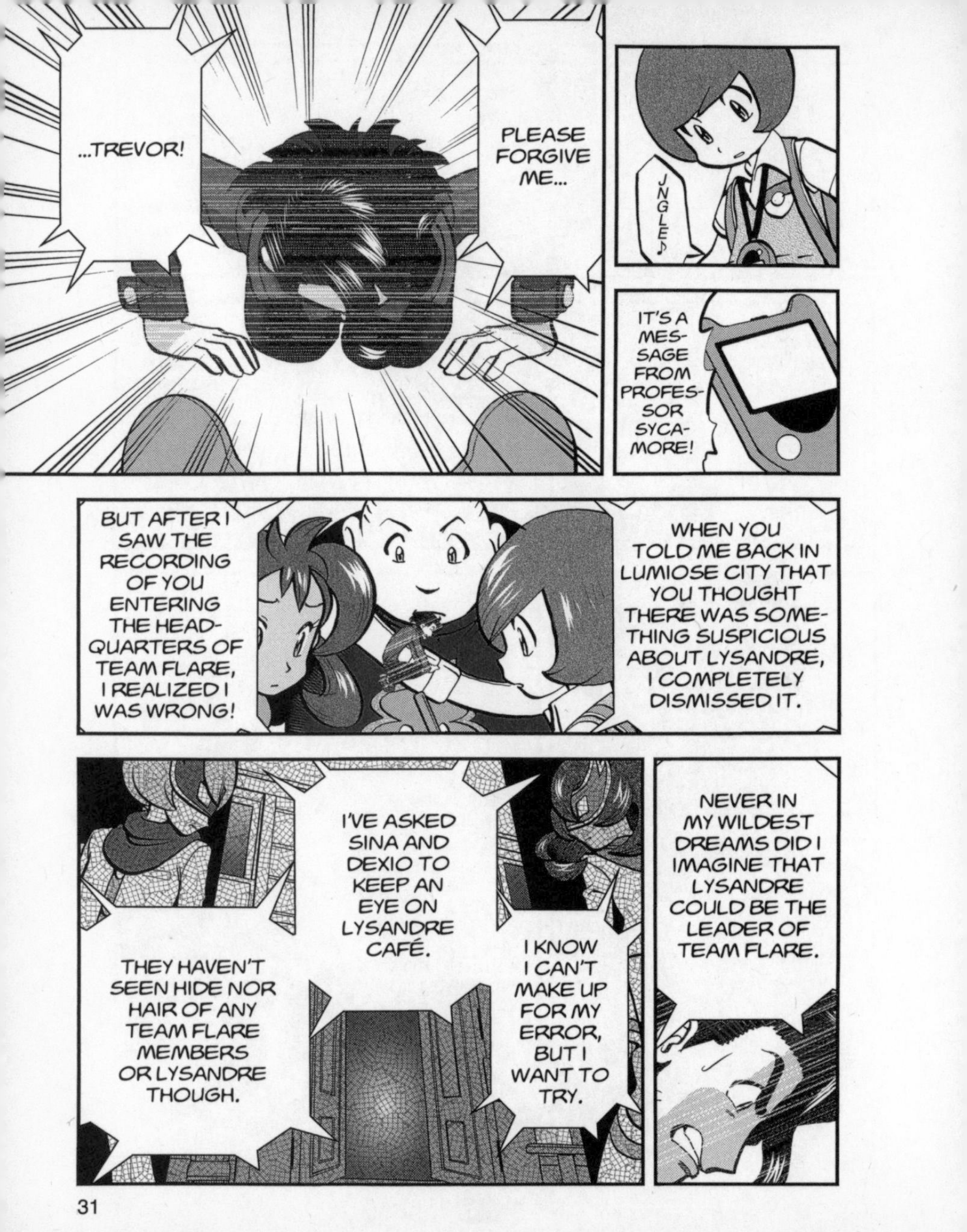
JNGLE♪
IT'S A MES-SAGE FROM PROFES-SOR SYCA-MORE!
PLEASE FORGIVE ME...
...TREVOR!
WHEN YOU TOLD ME BACK IN LUMIOSE CITY THAT YOU THOUGHT THERE WAS SOME-THING SUSPICIOUS ABOUT LYSANDRE, I COMPLETELY DISMISSED IT.
BUT AFTER I SAW THE RECORDING OF YOU ENTERING THE HEAD-QUARTERS OF TEAM FLARE, I REALIZED I WAS WRONG!
NEVER IN MY WILDEST DREAMS DID I IMAGINE THAT LYSANDRE COULD BE THE LEADER OF TEAM FLARE.
I KNOW I CAN'T MAKE UP FOR MY ERROR, BUT I WANT TO TRY.
I'VE ASKED SINA AND DEXIO TO KEEP AN EYE ON LYSANDRE CAFÉ.
THEY HAVEN'T SEEN HIDE NOR HAIR OF ANY TEAM FLARE MEMBERS OR LYSANDRE THOUGH.

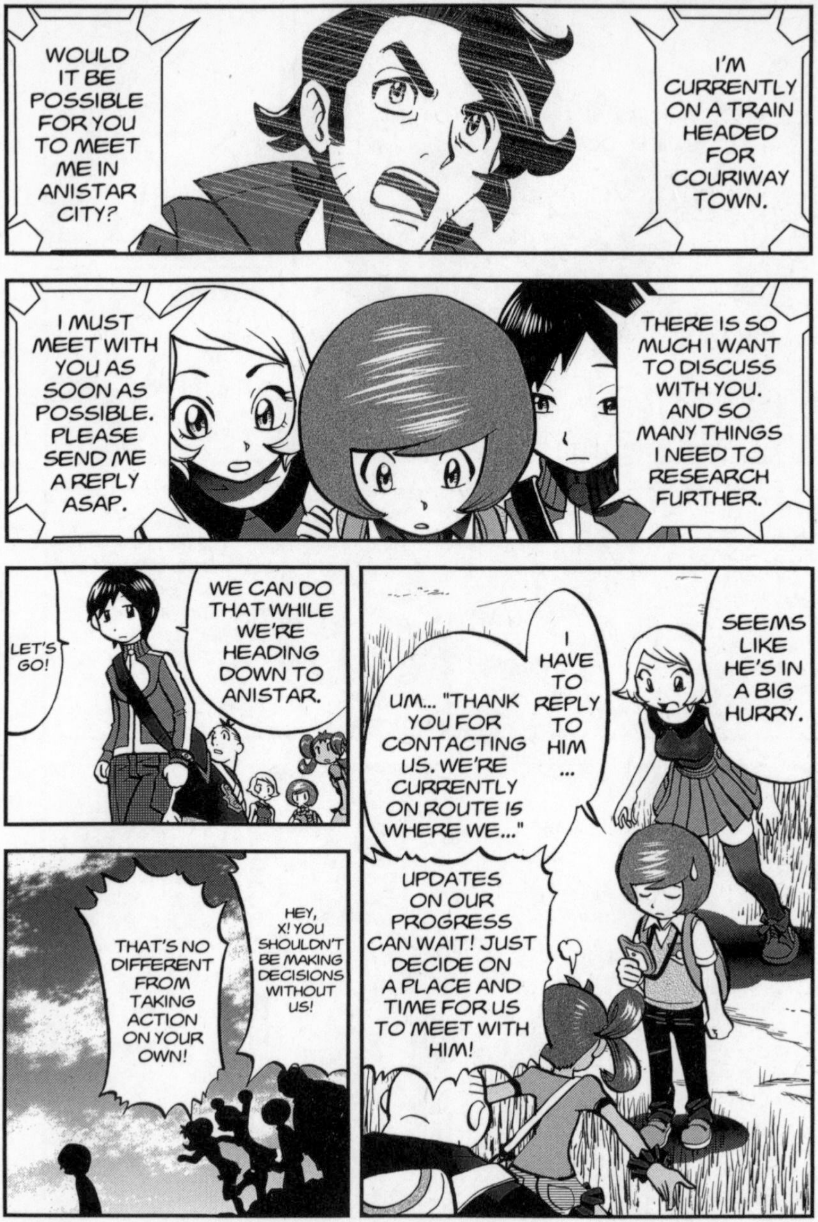
I'M CURRENTLY ON A TRAIN HEADED FOR COURIWAY TOWN.
WOULD IT BE POSSIBLE FOR YOU TO MEET ME IN ANISTAR CITY?
THERE IS SO MUCH I WANT TO DISCUSS WITH YOU. AND SO MANY THINGS I NEED TO RESEARCH FURTHER.
I MUST MEET WITH YOU AS SOON AS POSSIBLE. PLEASE SEND ME A REPLY ASAP.
SEEMS LIKE HE'S IN A BIG HURRY.
I HAVE TO REPLY TO HIM ...
UM... "THANK YOU FOR CONTACTING US. WE'RE CURRENTLY ON ROUTE 15 WHERE WE..."
UPDATES ON OUR PROGRESS CAN WAIT! JUST DECIDE ON A PLACE AND TIME FOR US TO MEET WITH HIM!
WE CAN DO THAT WHILE WE'RE HEADING DOWN TO ANISTAR.
LET'S GO!
HEY, X! YOU SHOULDN'T BE MAKING DECISIONS WITHOUT US!
THAT'S NO DIFFERENT FROM TAKING ACTION ON YOUR OWN!

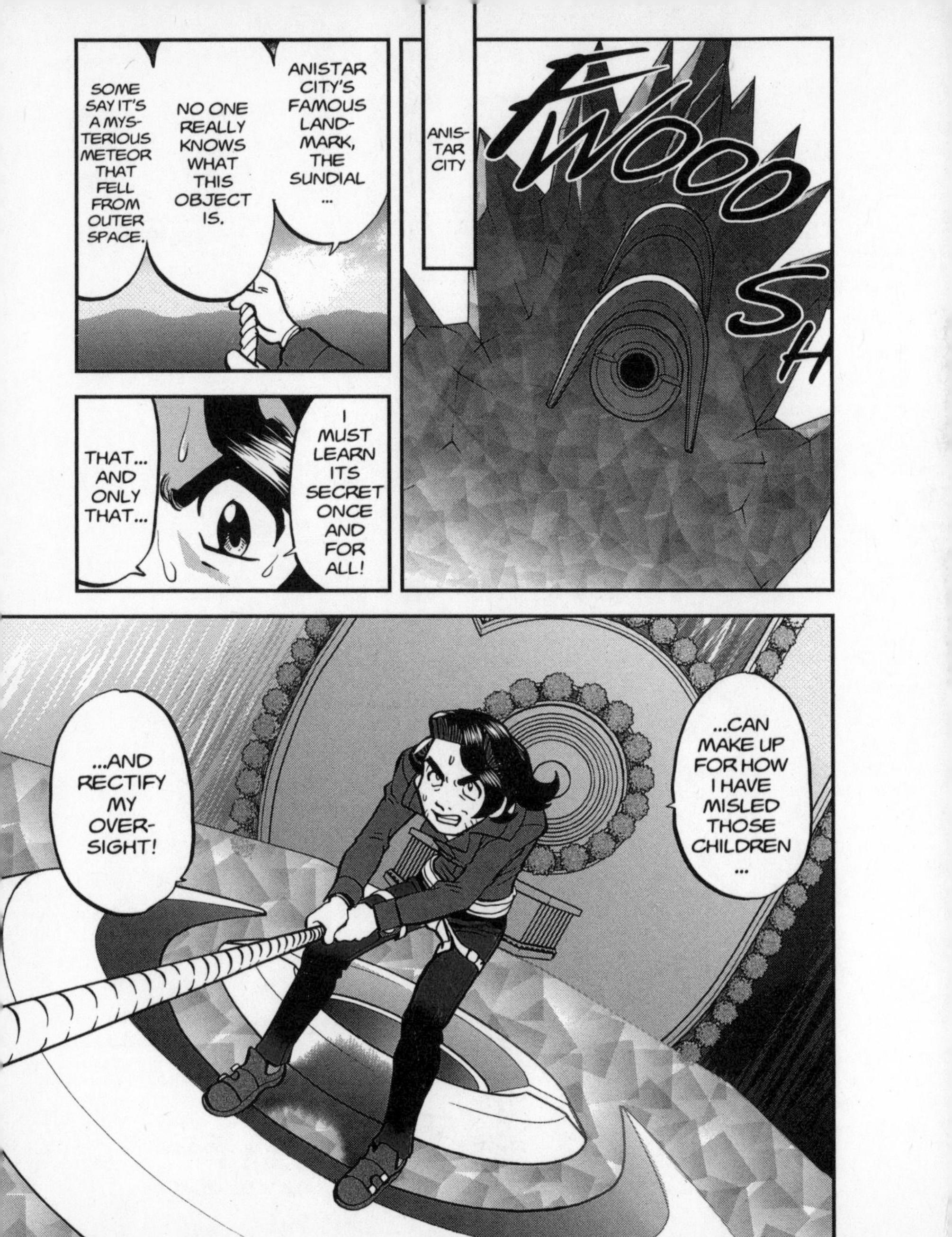
ANISTAR CITY
FWOOOSH
ANISTAR CITY'S FAMOUS LANDMARK, THE SUNDIAL...
NO ONE REALLY KNOWS WHAT THIS OBJECT IS.
SOME SAY IT'S A MYSTERIOUS METEOR THAT FELL FROM OUTER SPACE.
I MUST LEARN ITS SECRET ONCE AND FOR ALL!
THAT... AND ONLY THAT...
...CAN MAKE UP FOR HOW I HAVE MISLED THOSE CHILDREN...
...AND RECTIFY MY OVERSIGHT!

Current Location

Route 15
Brun Way

This path has become a popular
hangout for the wild and
directionless kids of Lumiose City.

Adventure 29 Hawlucha Attack

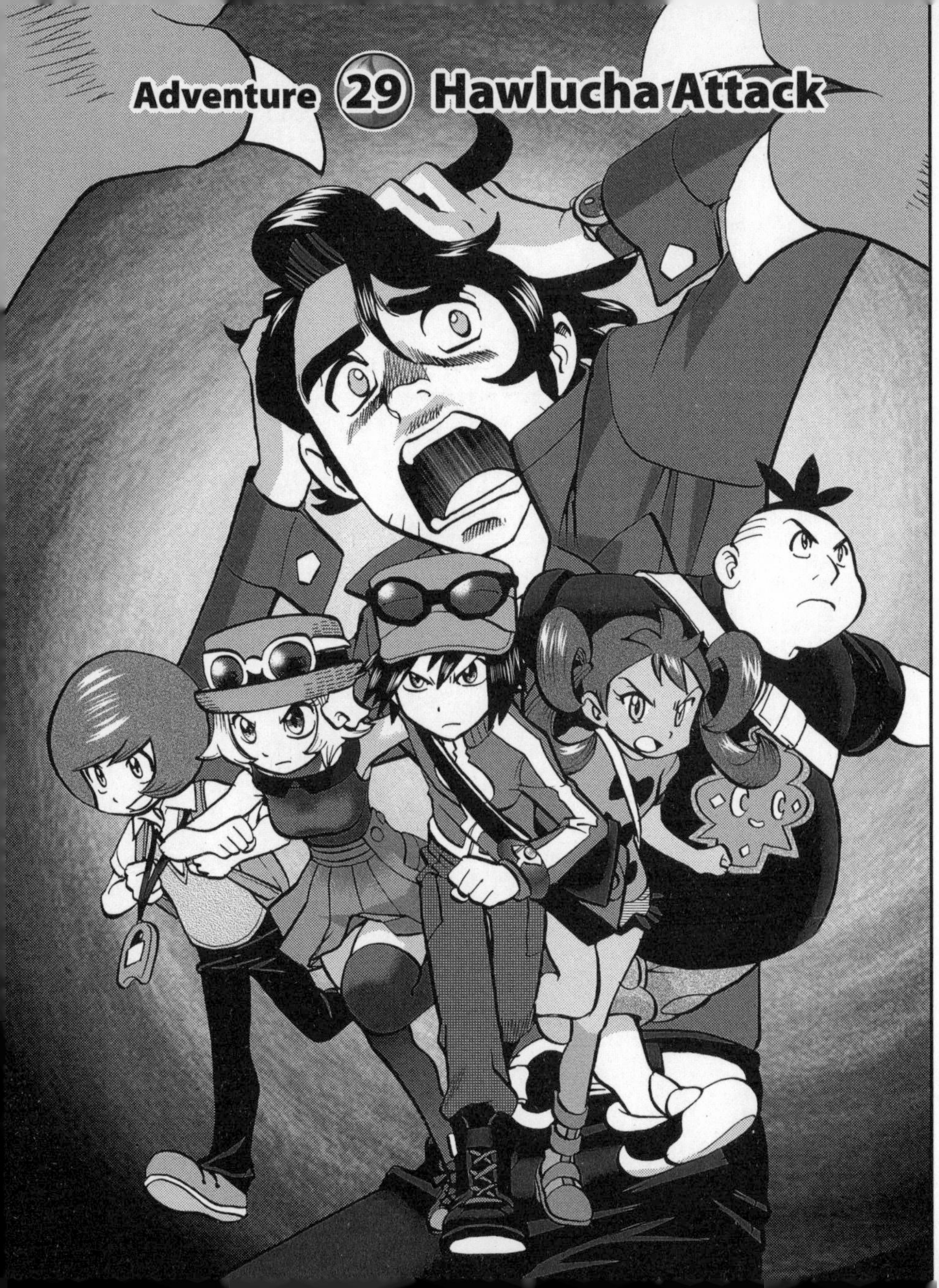

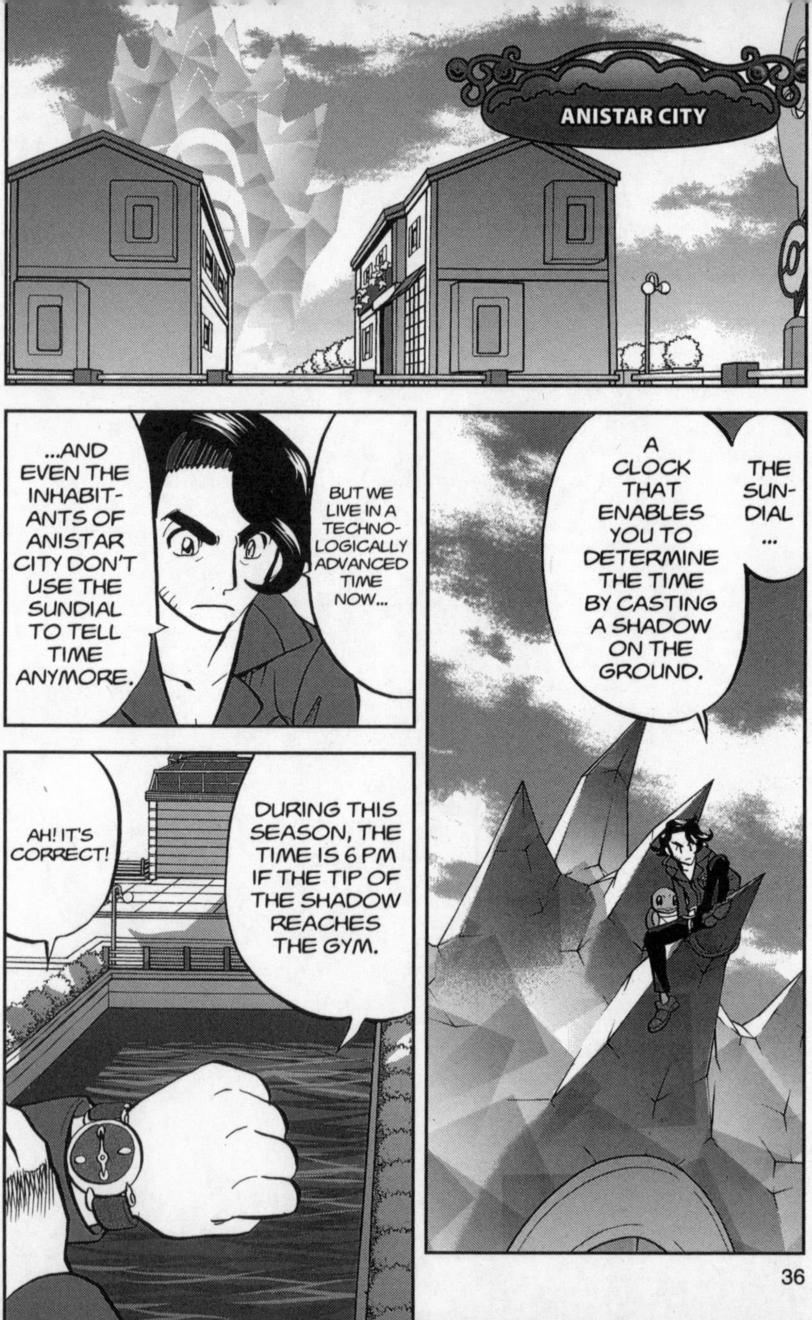
ANISTAR CITY
THE SUN-DIAL...
A CLOCK THAT ENABLES YOU TO DETERMINE THE TIME BY CASTING A SHADOW ON THE GROUND.
BUT WE LIVE IN A TECHNO-LOGICALLY ADVANCED TIME NOW...
...AND EVEN THE INHABIT-ANTS OF ANISTAR CITY DON'T USE THE SUNDIAL TO TELL TIME ANYMORE.
DURING THIS SEASON, THE TIME IS 6 PM IF THE TIP OF THE SHADOW REACHES THE GYM.
AH! IT'S CORRECT!

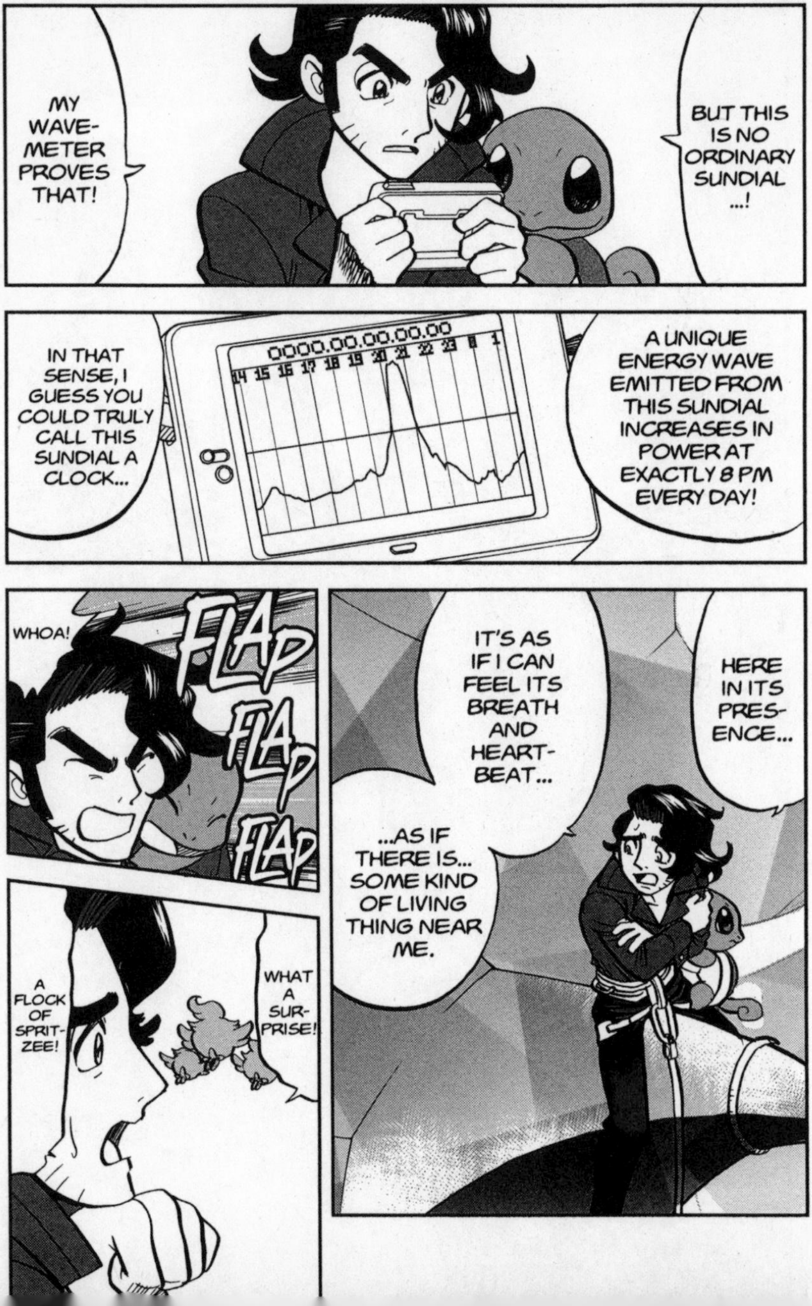
BUT THIS IS NO ORDINARY SUNDIAL ...!
MY WAVE-METER PROVES THAT!
A UNIQUE ENERGY WAVE EMITTED FROM THIS SUNDIAL INCREASES IN POWER AT EXACTLY 8 PM EVERY DAY!
0000.00.00.00.00
IN THAT SENSE, I GUESS YOU COULD TRULY CALL THIS SUNDIAL A CLOCK...
HERE IN ITS PRES-ENCE...
IT'S AS IF I CAN FEEL ITS BREATH AND HEART-BEAT...
...AS IF THERE IS... SOME KIND OF LIVING THING NEAR ME.
FLAP FLAP FLAP FLAP
WHOA!
WHAT A SUR-PRISE!
A FLOCK OF SPRIT-ZEE!

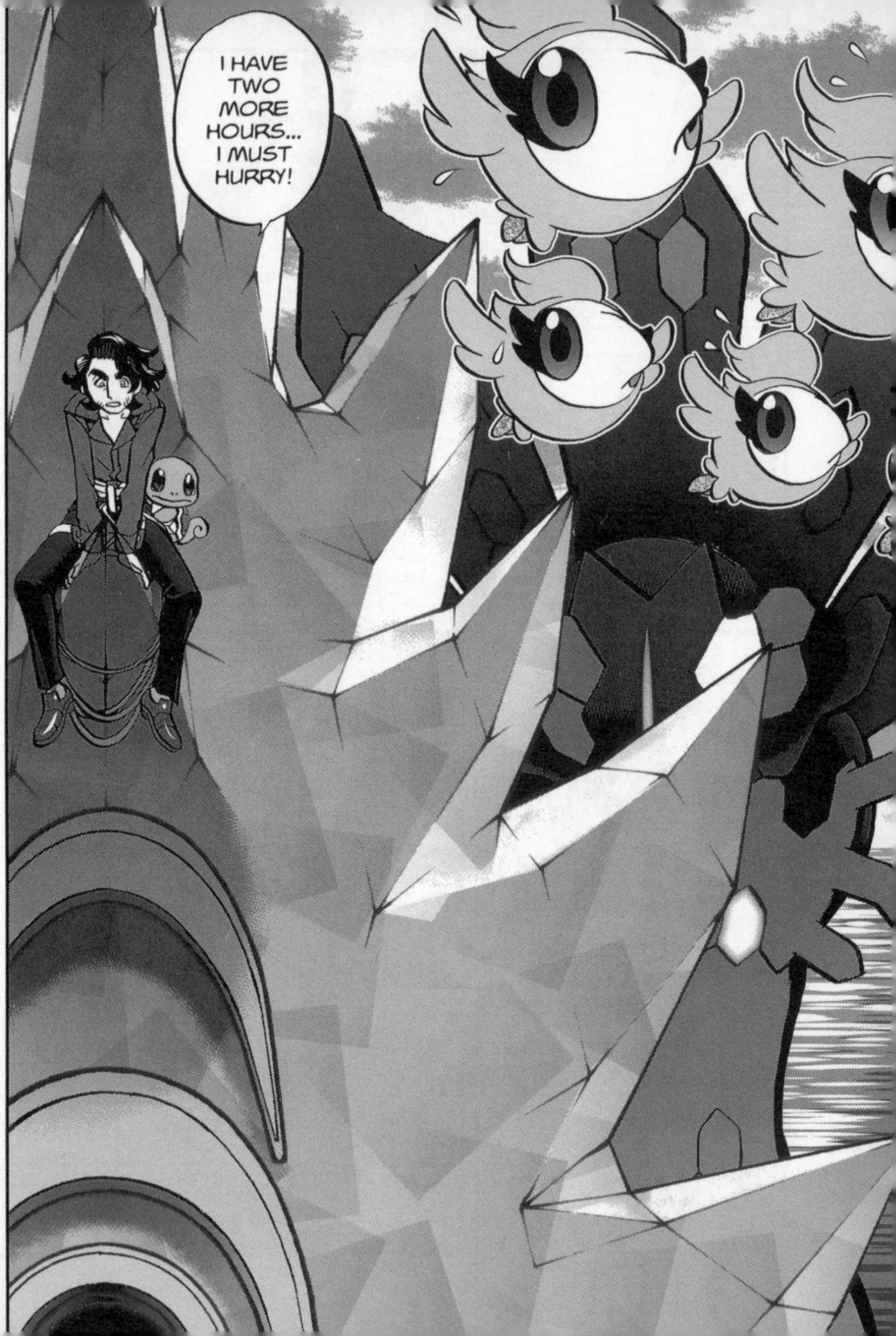
I HAVE TWO MORE HOURS... I MUST HURRY!

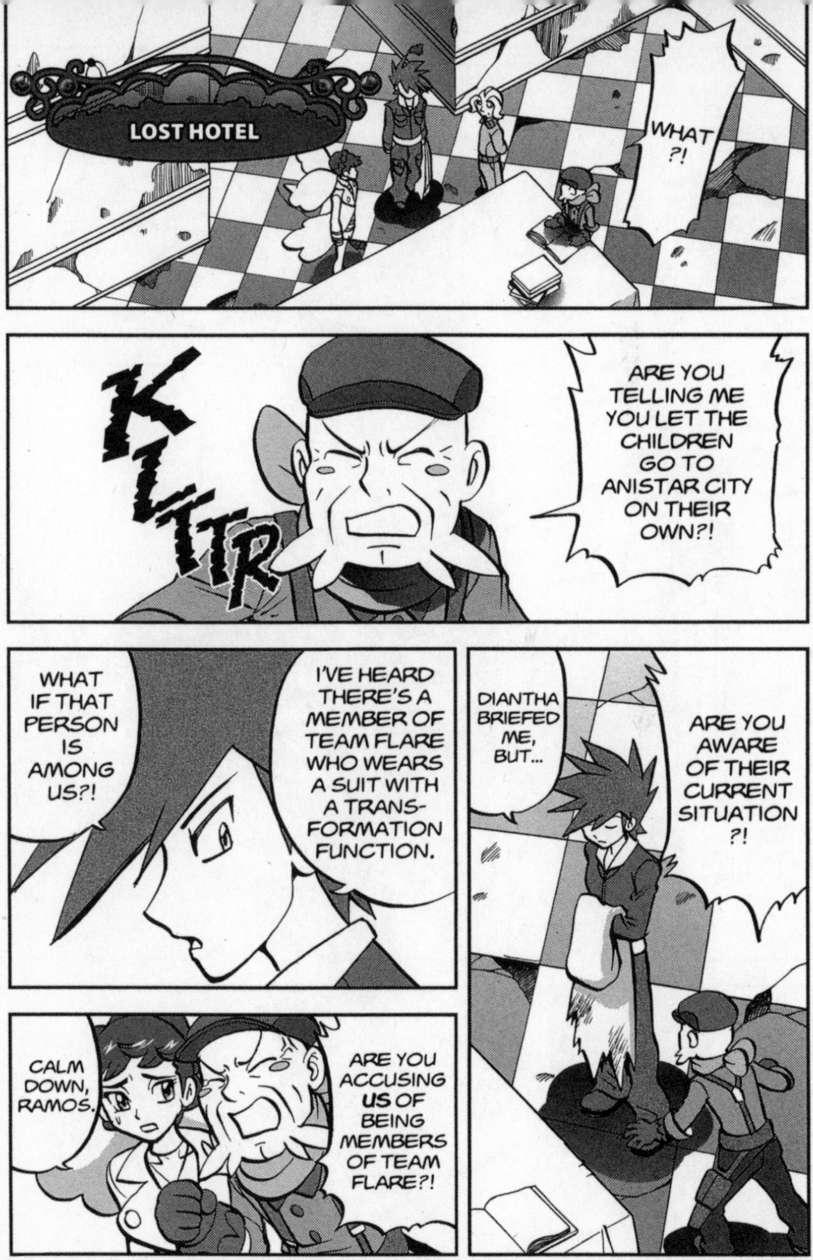
WHAT?!
LOST HOTEL
ARE YOU TELLING ME YOU LET THE CHILDREN GO TO ANISTAR CITY ON THEIR OWN?!
KLTTR
ARE YOU AWARE OF THEIR CURRENT SITUATION?!
DIANTHA BRIEFED ME, BUT...
I'VE HEARD THERE'S A MEMBER OF TEAM FLARE WHO WEARS A SUIT WITH A TRANS-FORMATION FUNCTION.
WHAT IF THAT PERSON IS AMONG US?!
ARE YOU ACCUSING **US** OF BEING MEMBERS OF TEAM FLARE?!
CALM DOWN, RAMOS.

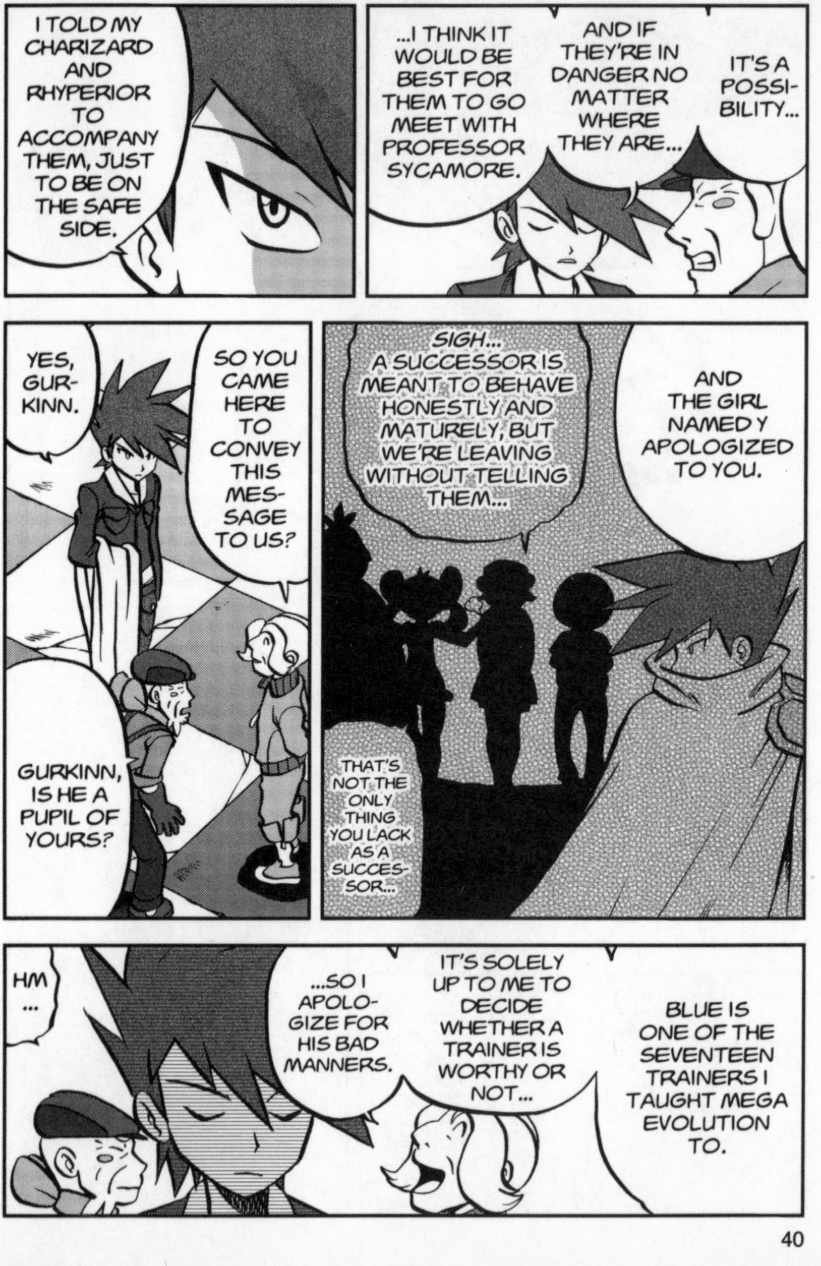
IT'S A POSSIBILITY...
AND IF THEY'RE IN DANGER NO MATTER WHERE THEY ARE...
...I THINK IT WOULD BE BEST FOR THEM TO GO MEET WITH PROFESSOR SYCAMORE.
I TOLD MY CHARIZARD AND RHYPERIOR TO ACCOMPANY THEM, JUST TO BE ON THE SAFE SIDE.
AND THE GIRL NAMED Y APOLOGIZED TO YOU.
SIGH... A SUCCESSOR IS MEANT TO BEHAVE HONESTLY AND MATURELY, BUT WE'RE LEAVING WITHOUT TELLING THEM...
THAT'S NOT THE ONLY THING YOU LACK AS A SUCCESSOR...
SO YOU CAME HERE TO CONVEY THIS MESSAGE TO US?
YES, GURKINN.
GURKINN, IS HE A PUPIL OF YOURS?
BLUE IS ONE OF THE SEVENTEEN TRAINERS I TAUGHT MEGA EVOLUTION TO.
IT'S SOLELY UP TO ME TO DECIDE WHETHER A TRAINER IS WORTHY OR NOT...
...SO I APOLOGIZE FOR HIS BAD MANNERS.
HM...

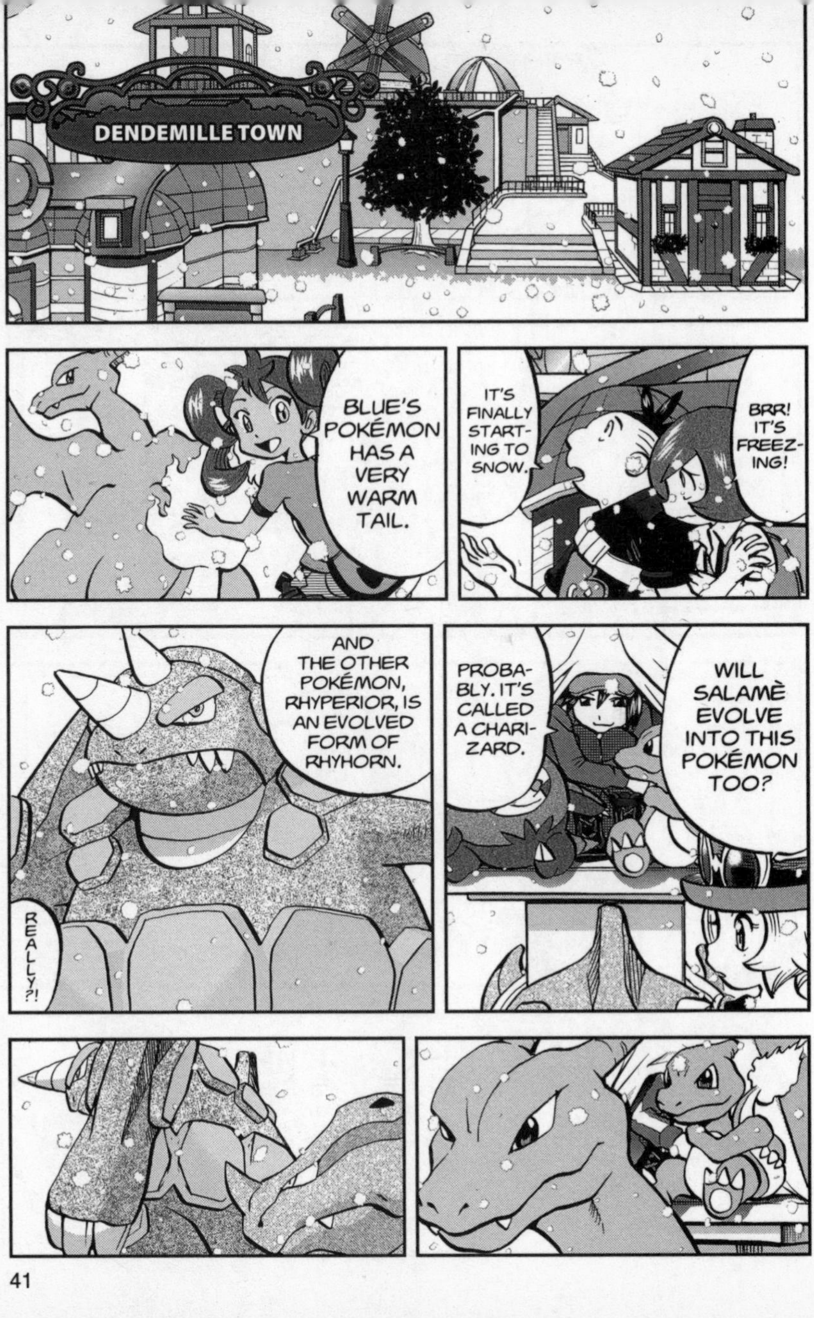
DENDEMILLE TOWN
BRR! IT'S FREEZING!
IT'S FINALLY STARTING TO SNOW.
BLUE'S POKÉMON HAS A VERY WARM TAIL.
WILL SALAMÈ EVOLVE INTO THIS POKÉMON TOO?
PROBABLY. IT'S CALLED A CHARIZARD.
AND THE OTHER POKÉMON, RHYPERIOR, IS AN EVOLVED FORM OF RHYHORN.
REALLY?!

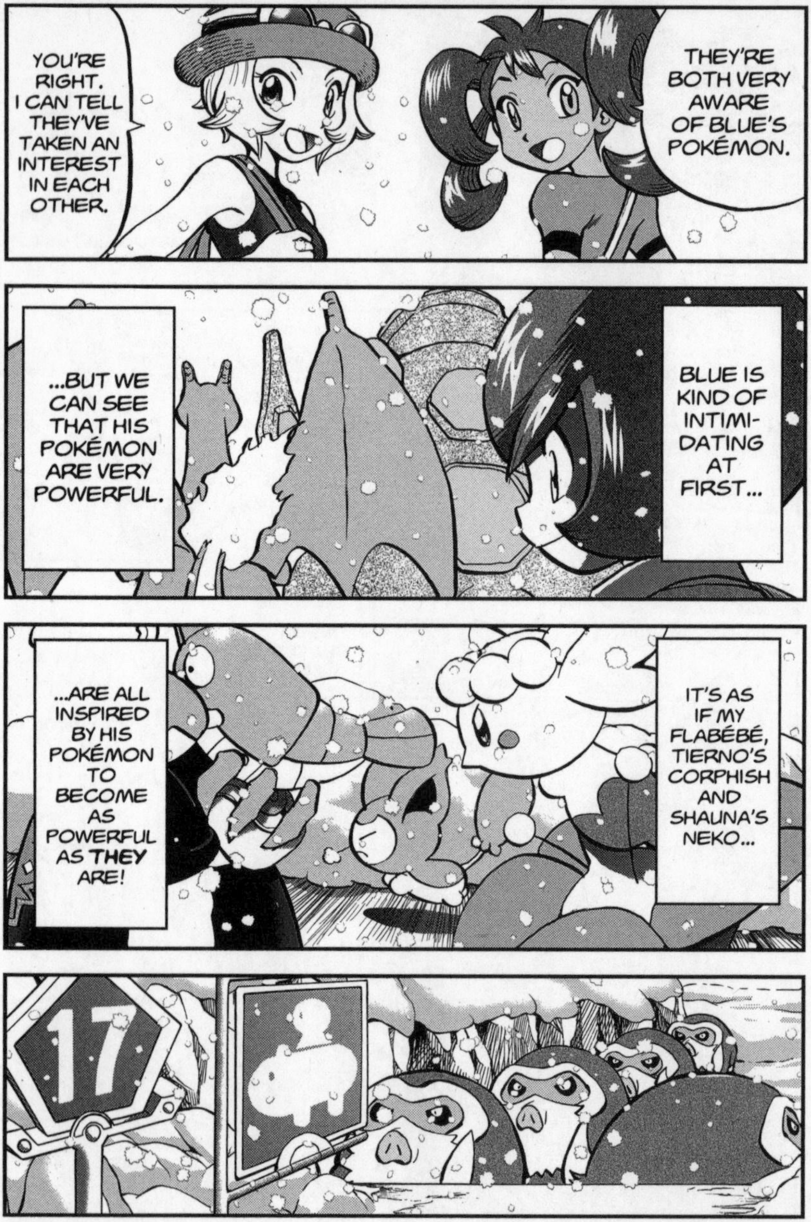
THEY'RE BOTH VERY AWARE OF BLUE'S POKÉMON.
YOU'RE RIGHT. I CAN TELL THEY'VE TAKEN AN INTEREST IN EACH OTHER.
BLUE IS KIND OF INTIMI-DATING AT FIRST...
...BUT WE CAN SEE THAT HIS POKÉMON ARE VERY POWERFUL.
IT'S AS IF MY FLABÉBÉ, TIERNO'S CORPHISH AND SHAUNA'S NEKO...
...ARE ALL INSPIRED BY HIS POKÉMON TO BECOME AS POWERFUL AS **THEY** ARE!
17

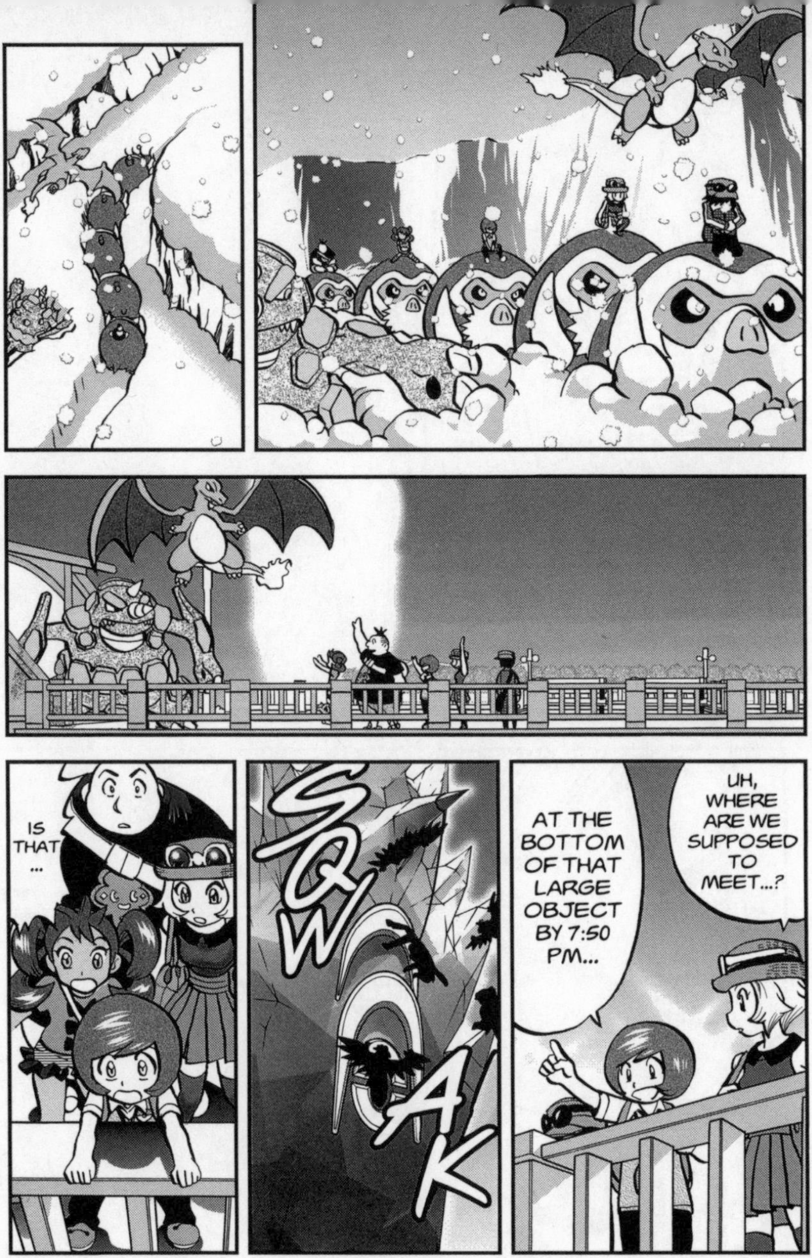
UH, WHERE ARE WE SUPPOSED TO MEET...?
AT THE BOTTOM OF THAT LARGE OBJECT BY 7:50 PM...
SQWAK
IS THAT...

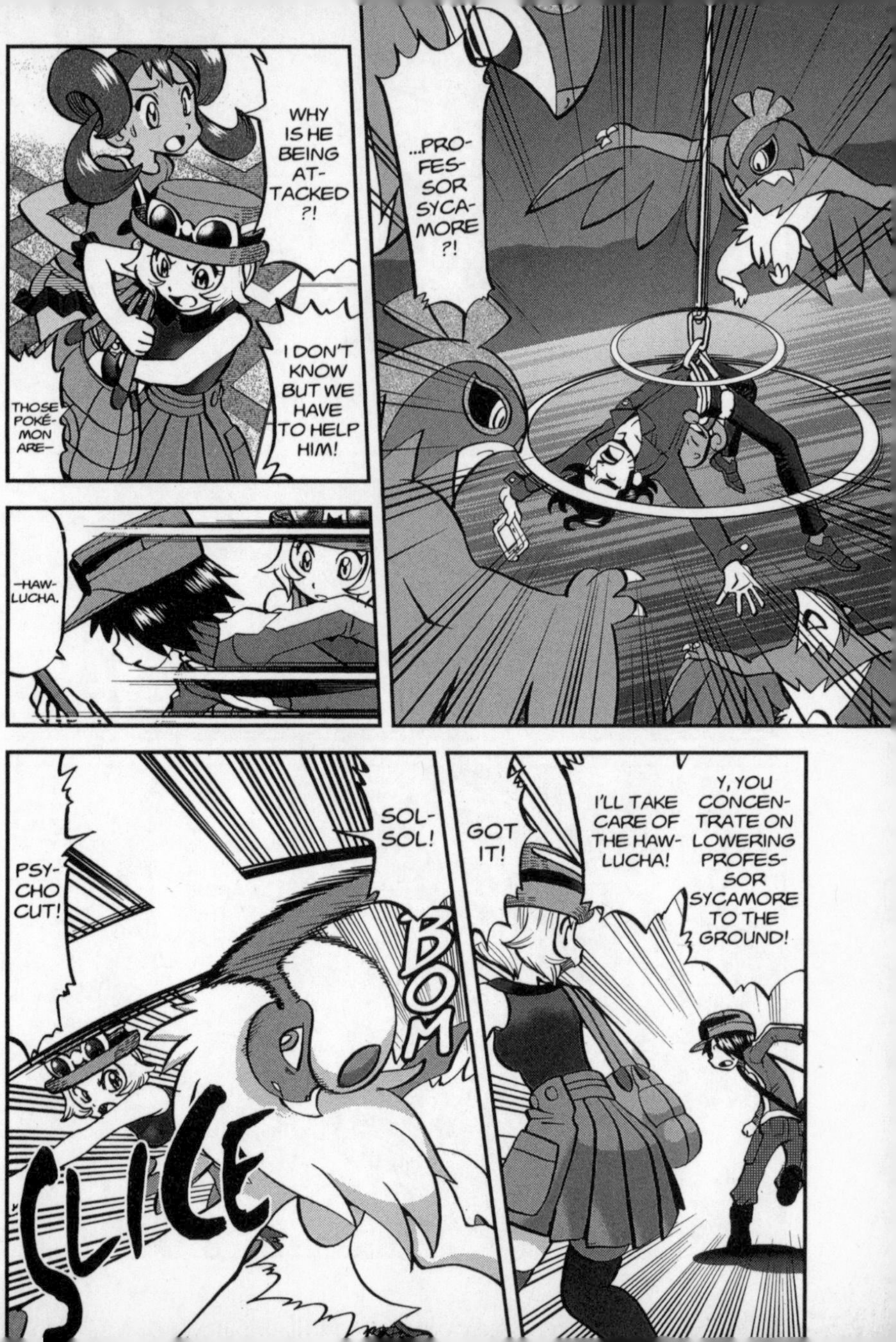
...PROFESSOR SYCAMORE?!
WHY IS HE BEING ATTACKED?!
I DON'T KNOW BUT WE HAVE TO HELP HIM!
THOSE POKÉMON ARE—
—HAWLUCHA.
Y, YOU CONCENTRATE ON LOWERING PROFESSOR SYCAMORE TO THE GROUND!
I'LL TAKE CARE OF THE HAWLUCHA!
GOT IT!
SOL-SOL!
PSYCHO CUT!
BOM
SLICE

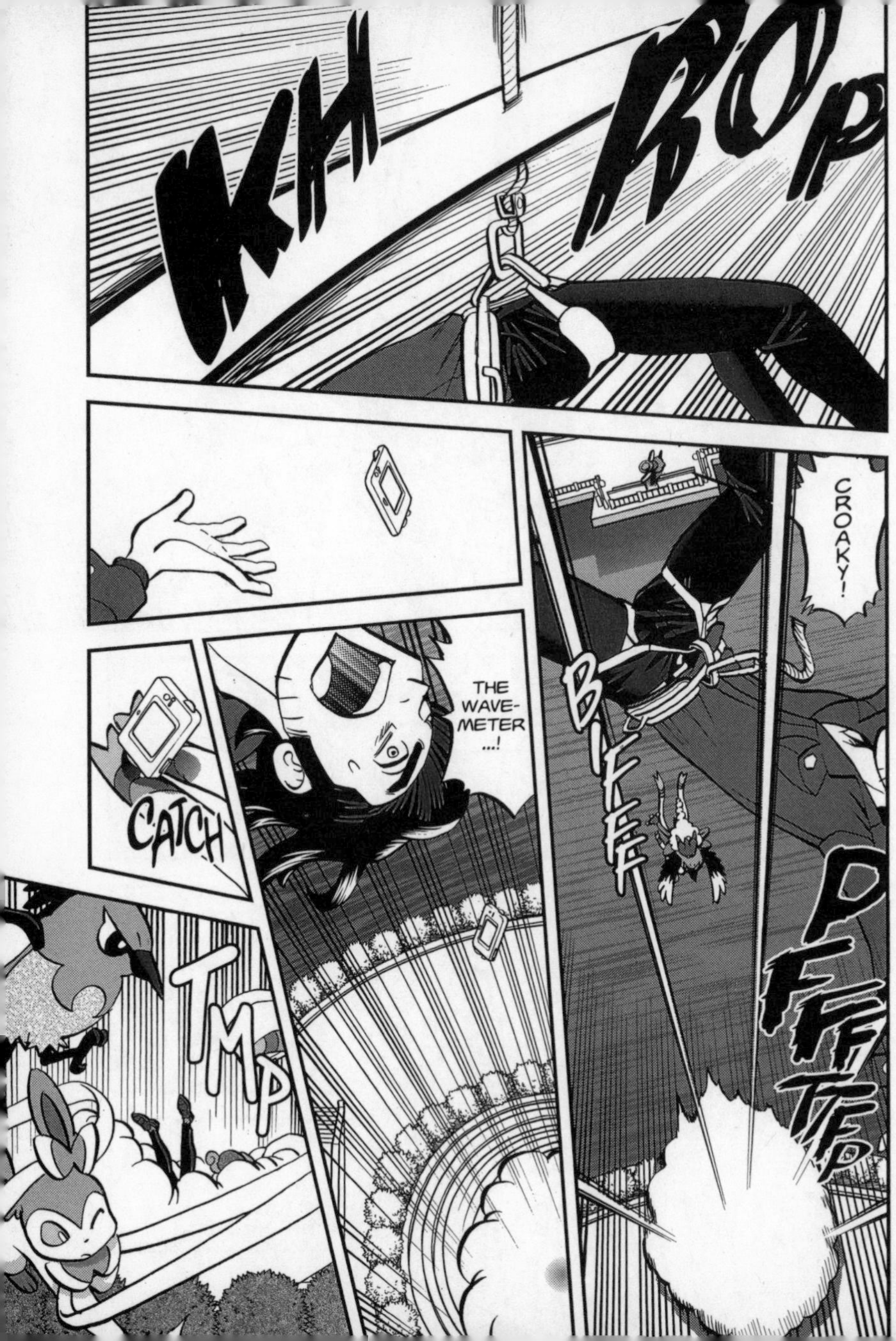
KHROP
CROAKY!
BIFFF
PFFFTFP
THE WAVE-METER ...!
CATCH
TMP

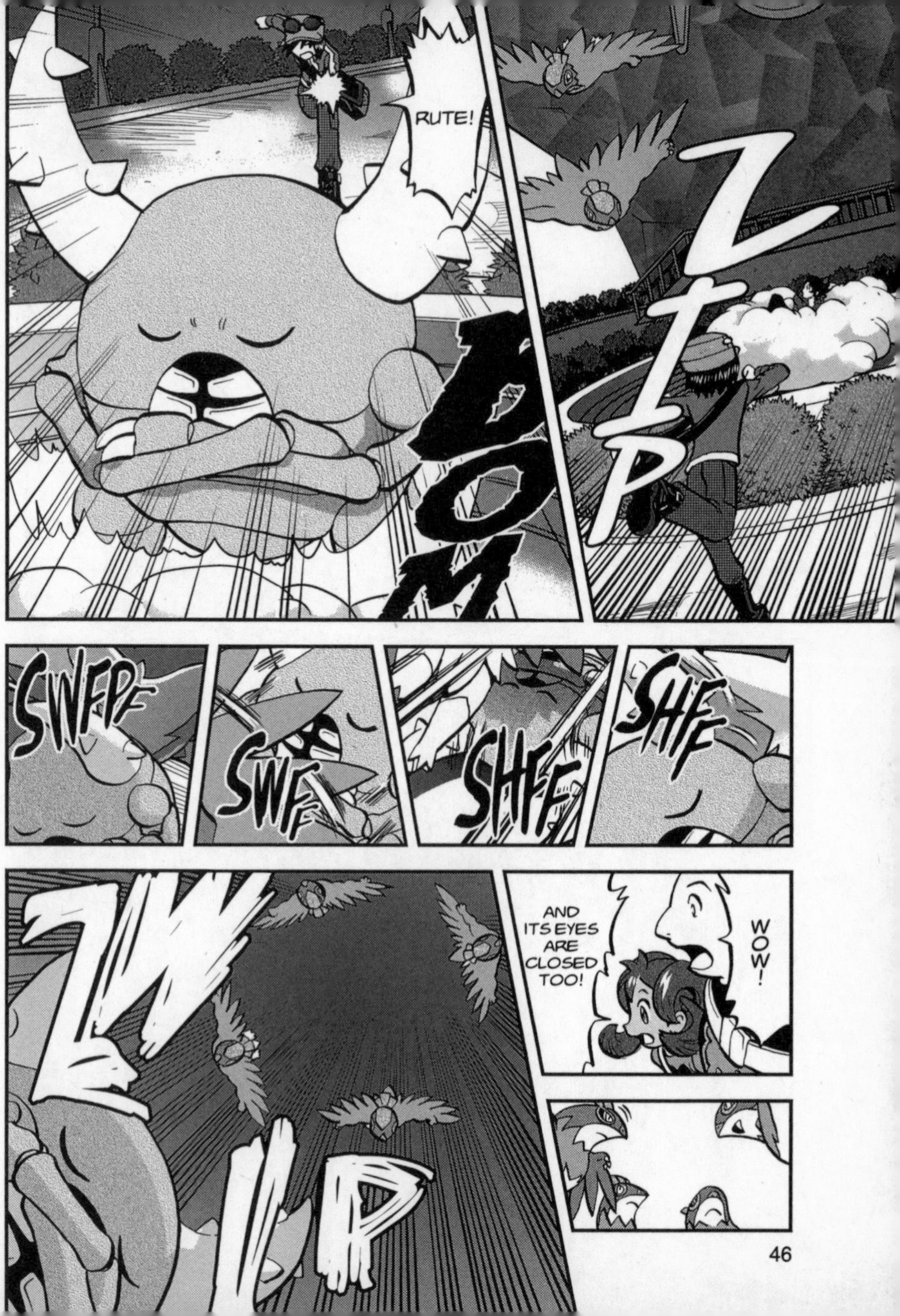
ZIIP
RUTE!
BOM
SHFF
SHFF
SWF
SWFPF
WOW!
AND ITS EYES ARE CLOSED TOO!
ZWIP

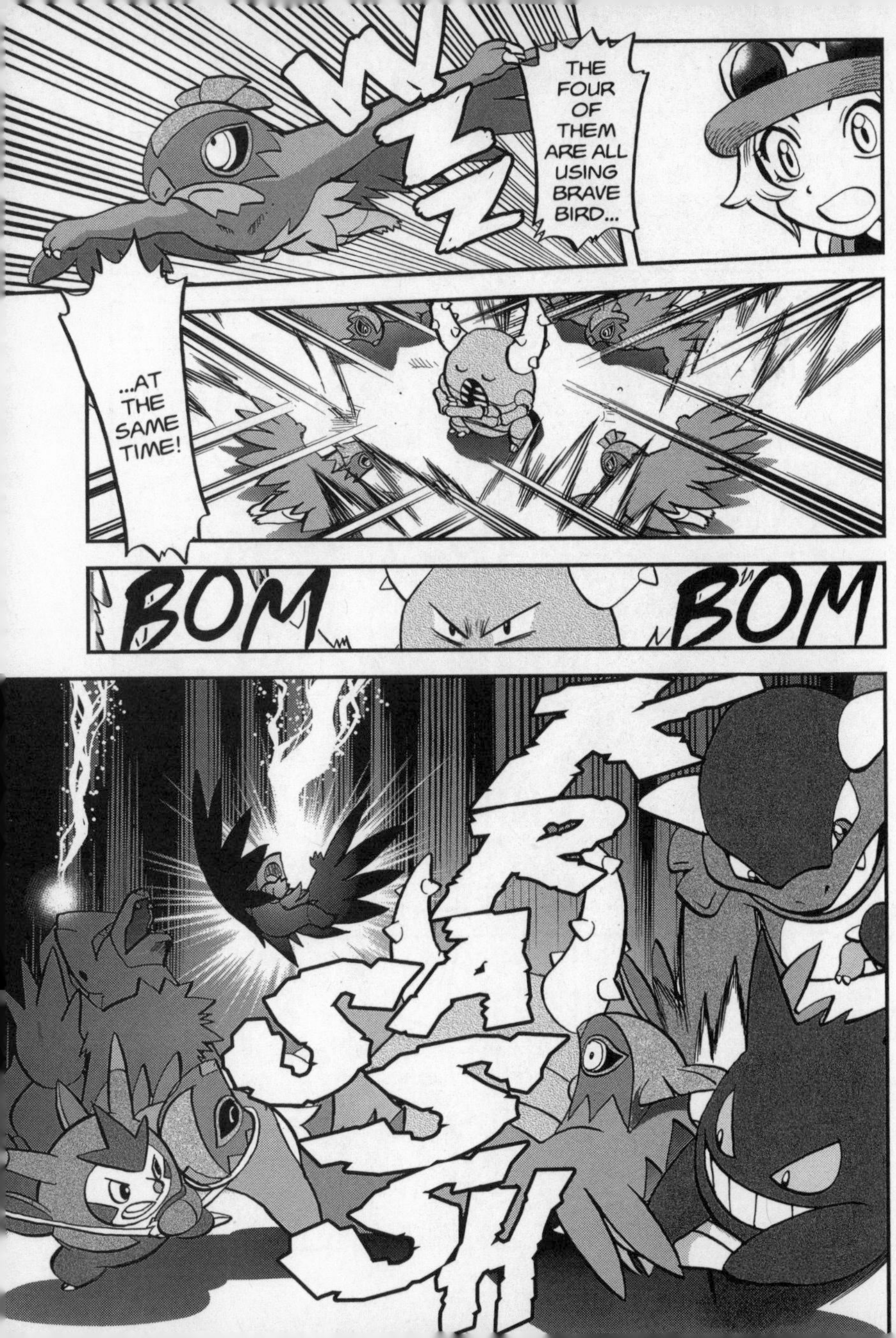
WZZ
THE FOUR OF THEM ARE ALL USING BRAVE BIRD...
...AT THE SAME TIME!
BOM
BOM

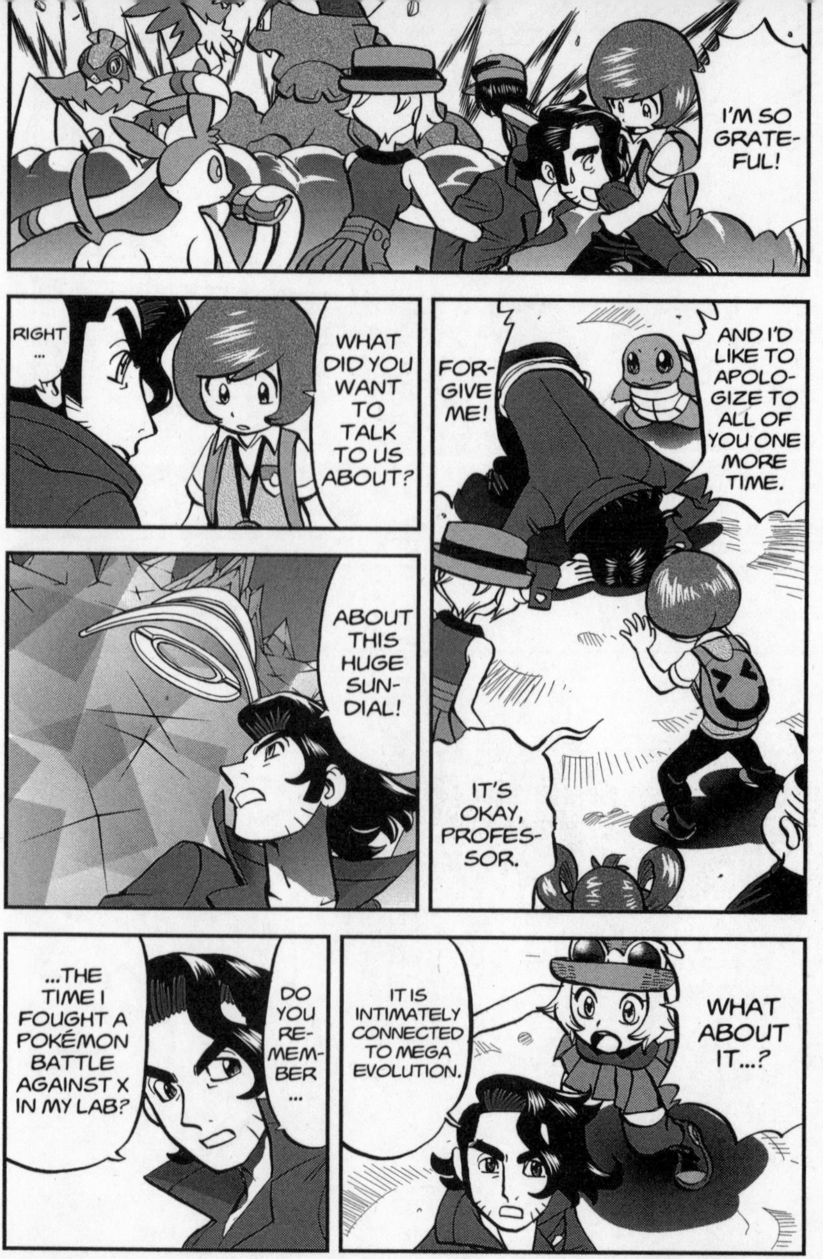
I'M SO GRATE-FUL!
AND I'D LIKE TO APOLO-GIZE TO ALL OF YOU ONE MORE TIME.
FOR-GIVE ME!
IT'S OKAY, PROFES-SOR.
WHAT DID YOU WANT TO TALK TO US ABOUT?
RIGHT ...
ABOUT THIS HUGE SUN-DIAL!
WHAT ABOUT IT...?
IT IS INTIMATELY CONNECTED TO MEGA EVOLUTION.
DO YOU RE-MEM-BER ...
...THE TIME I FOUGHT A POKÉMON BATTLE AGAINST X IN MY LAB?

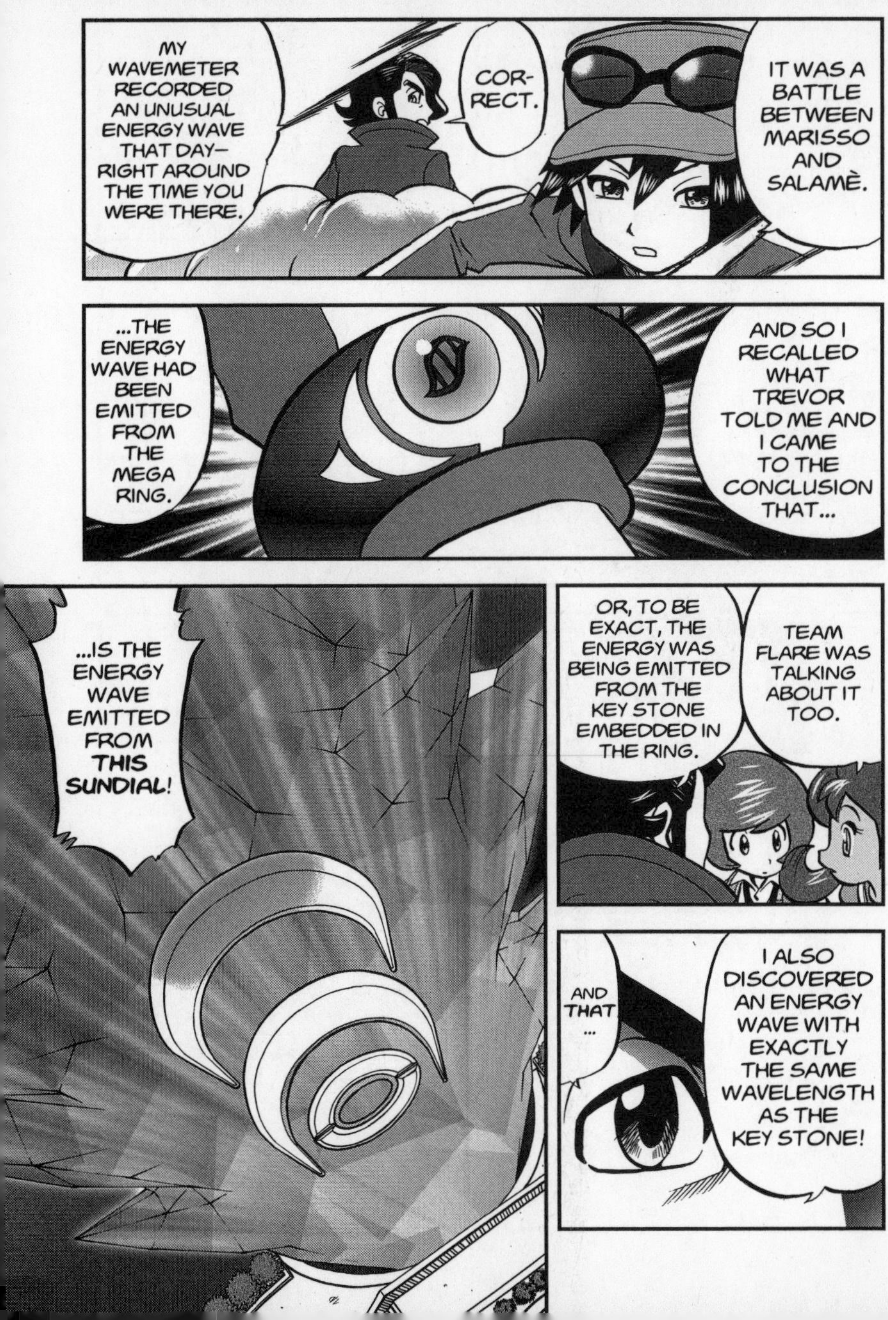
IT WAS A BATTLE BETWEEN MARISSO AND SALAMÈ.
COR-RECT.
MY WAVEMETER RECORDED AN UNUSUAL ENERGY WAVE THAT DAY—RIGHT AROUND THE TIME YOU WERE THERE.
AND SO I RECALLED WHAT TREVOR TOLD ME AND I CAME TO THE CONCLUSION THAT...
...THE ENERGY WAVE HAD BEEN EMITTED FROM THE MEGA RING.
TEAM FLARE WAS TALKING ABOUT IT TOO.
OR, TO BE EXACT, THE ENERGY WAS BEING EMITTED FROM THE KEY STONE EMBEDDED IN THE RING.
I ALSO DISCOVERED AN ENERGY WAVE WITH EXACTLY THE SAME WAVELENGTH AS THE KEY STONE!
AND THAT...
...IS THE ENERGY WAVE EMITTED FROM **THIS SUNDIAL**!

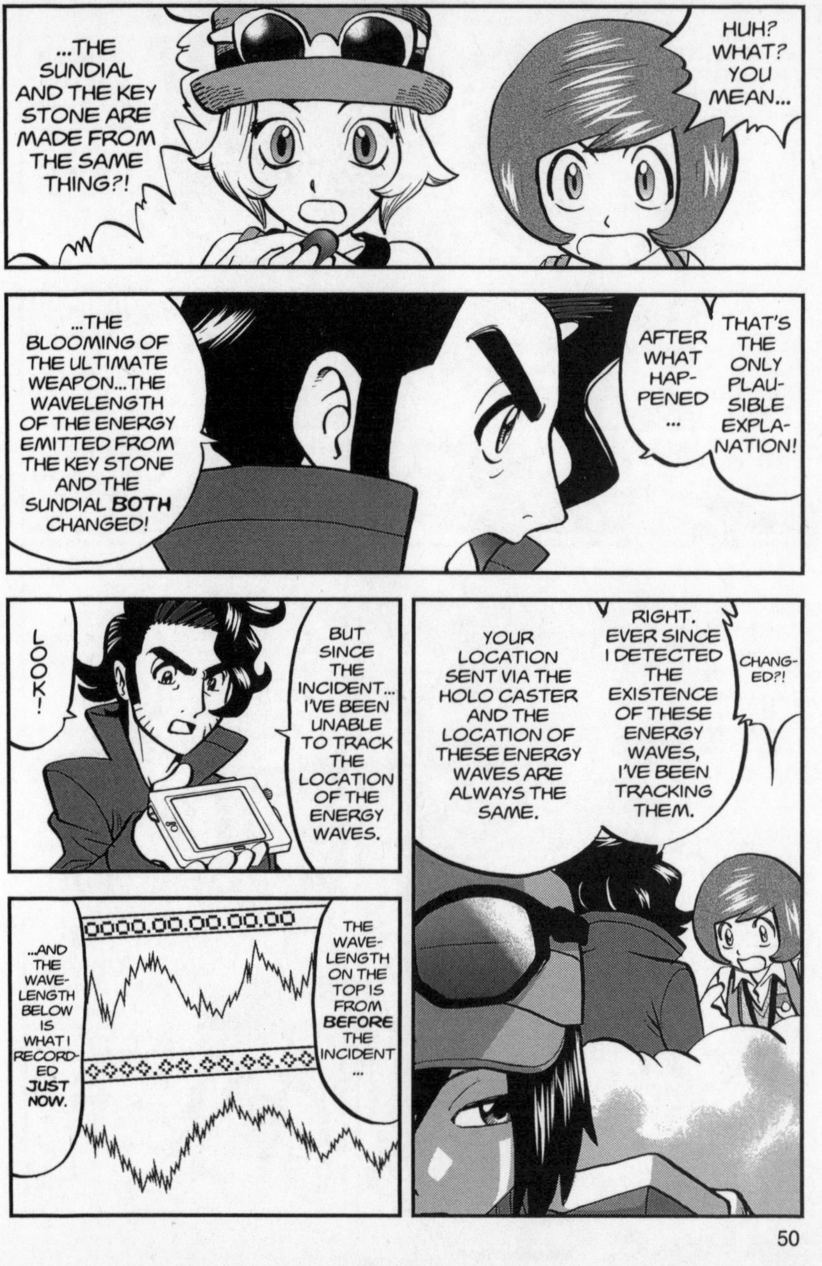
HUH? WHAT? YOU MEAN...
...THE SUNDIAL AND THE KEY STONE ARE MADE FROM THE SAME THING?!
THAT'S THE ONLY PLAU-SIBLE EXPLA-NATION!
AFTER WHAT HAP-PENED ...
...THE BLOOMING OF THE ULTIMATE WEAPON...THE WAVELENGTH OF THE ENERGY EMITTED FROM THE KEY STONE AND THE SUNDIAL **BOTH** CHANGED!
CHANG-ED?!
RIGHT. EVER SINCE I DETECTED THE EXISTENCE OF THESE ENERGY WAVES, I'VE BEEN TRACKING THEM.
YOUR LOCATION SENT VIA THE HOLO CASTER AND THE LOCATION OF THESE ENERGY WAVES ARE ALWAYS THE SAME.
BUT SINCE THE INCIDENT... I'VE BEEN UNABLE TO TRACK THE LOCATION OF THE ENERGY WAVES.
LOOK!
0000.00.00.00.00
THE WAVE-LENGTH ON THE TOP IS FROM **BEFORE** THE INCIDENT ...
...AND THE WAVE-LENGTH BELOW IS WHAT I RECORD-ED **JUST NOW.**
◇◇◇◇.◇◇.◇◇.◇◇.◇◇

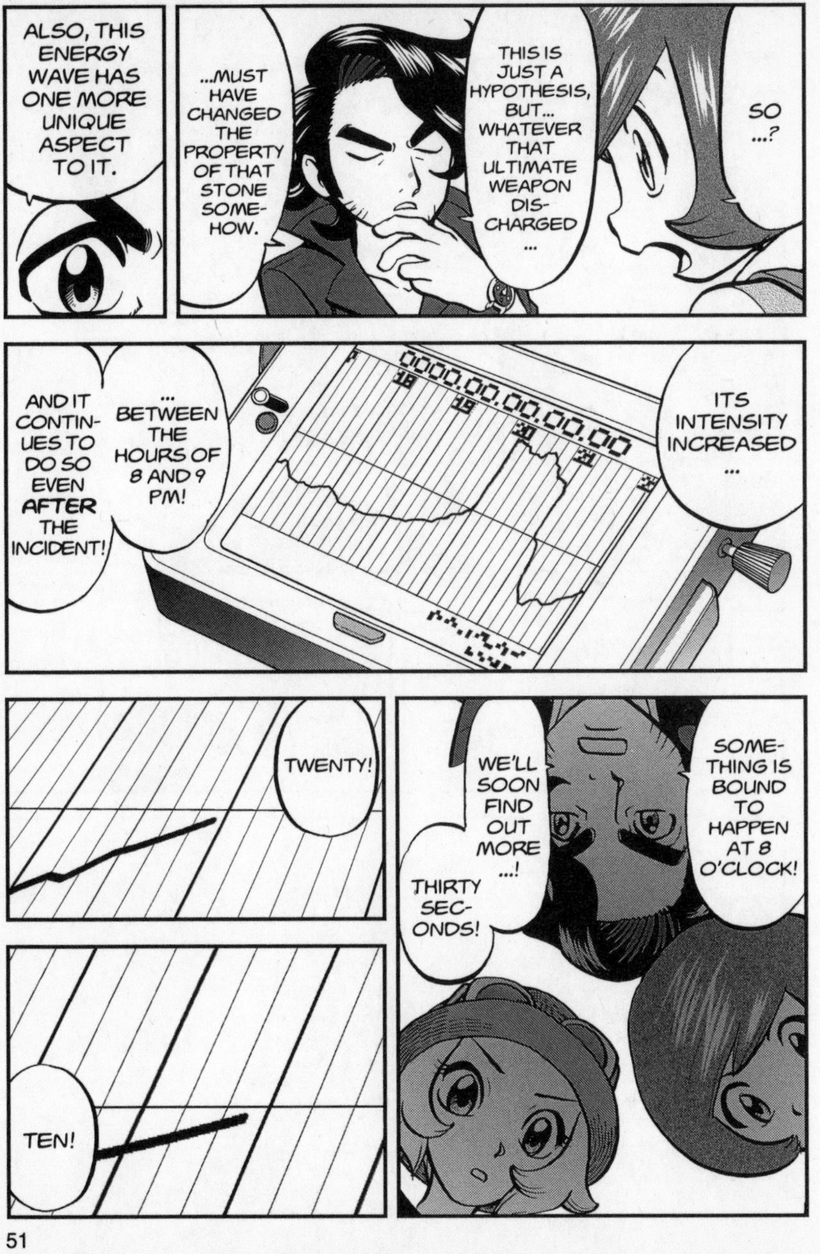
SO ...?
THIS IS JUST A HYPOTHESIS, BUT... WHATEVER THAT ULTIMATE WEAPON DIS-CHARGED ...
...MUST HAVE CHANGED THE PROPERTY OF THAT STONE SOME-HOW.
ALSO, THIS ENERGY WAVE HAS ONE MORE UNIQUE ASPECT TO IT.
ITS INTENSITY INCREASED ...
... BETWEEN THE HOURS OF 8 AND 9 PM!
AND IT CONTIN-UES TO DO SO EVEN **AFTER** THE INCIDENT!
SOME-THING IS BOUND TO HAPPEN AT 8 O'CLOCK!
WE'LL SOON FIND OUT MORE ...!
THIRTY SEC-ONDS!
TWENTY!
TEN!

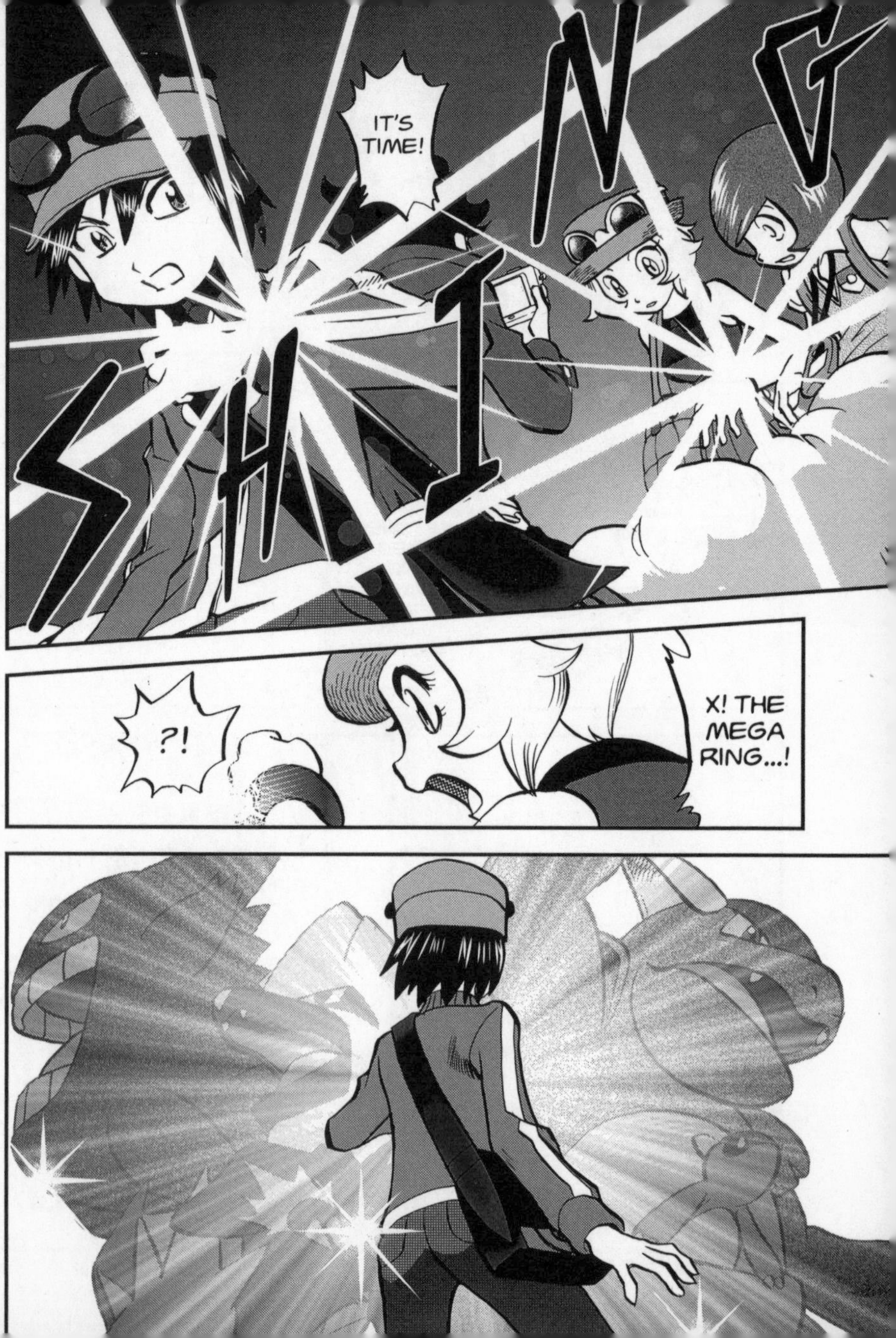
SHING
IT'S TIME!
X! THE MEGA RING...!
?!

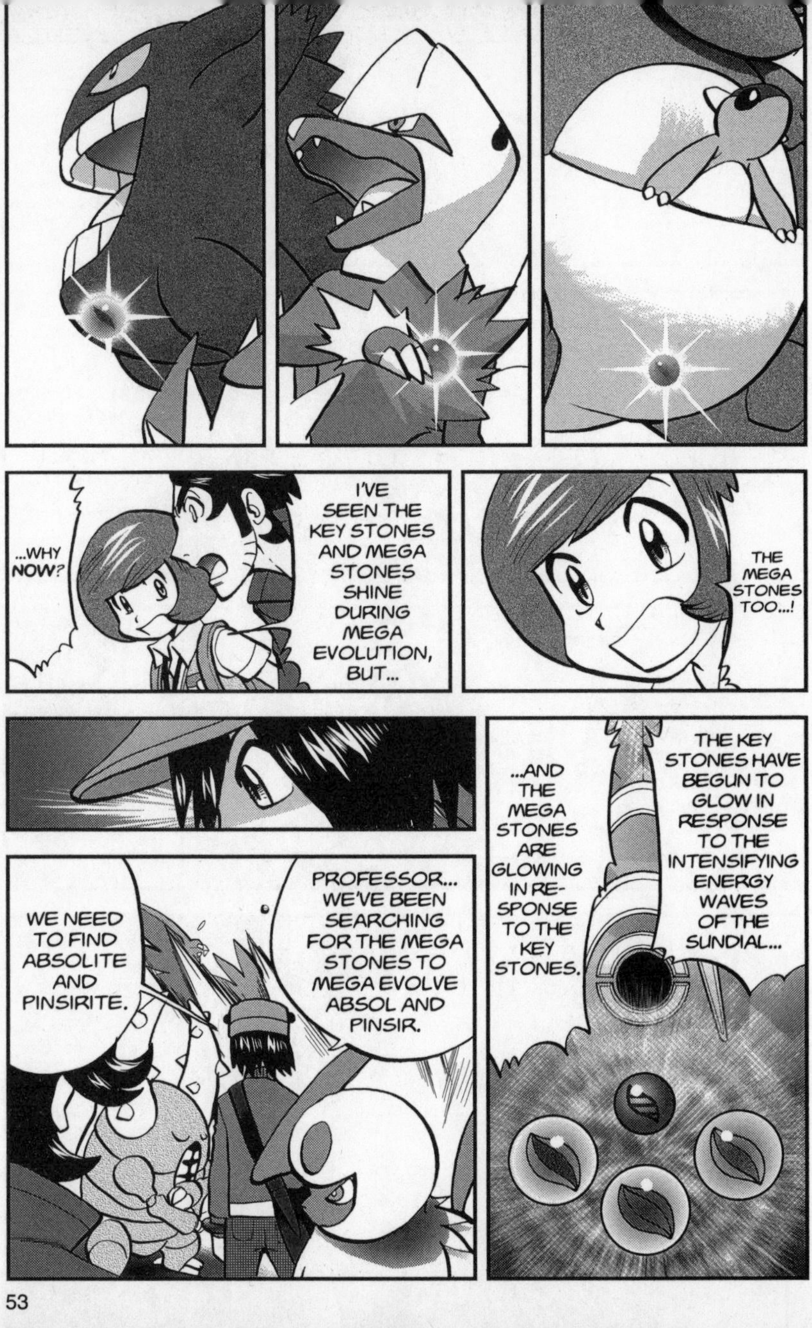
THE MEGA STONES TOO...!
I'VE SEEN THE KEY STONES AND MEGA STONES SHINE DURING MEGA EVOLUTION, BUT...
...WHY NOW?
THE KEY STONES HAVE BEGUN TO GLOW IN RESPONSE TO THE INTENSIFYING ENERGY WAVES OF THE SUNDIAL...
...AND THE MEGA STONES ARE GLOWING IN RE-SPONSE TO THE KEY STONES.
PROFESSOR... WE'VE BEEN SEARCHING FOR THE MEGA STONES TO MEGA EVOLVE ABSOL AND PINSIR.
WE NEED TO FIND ABSOLITE AND PINSIRITE.

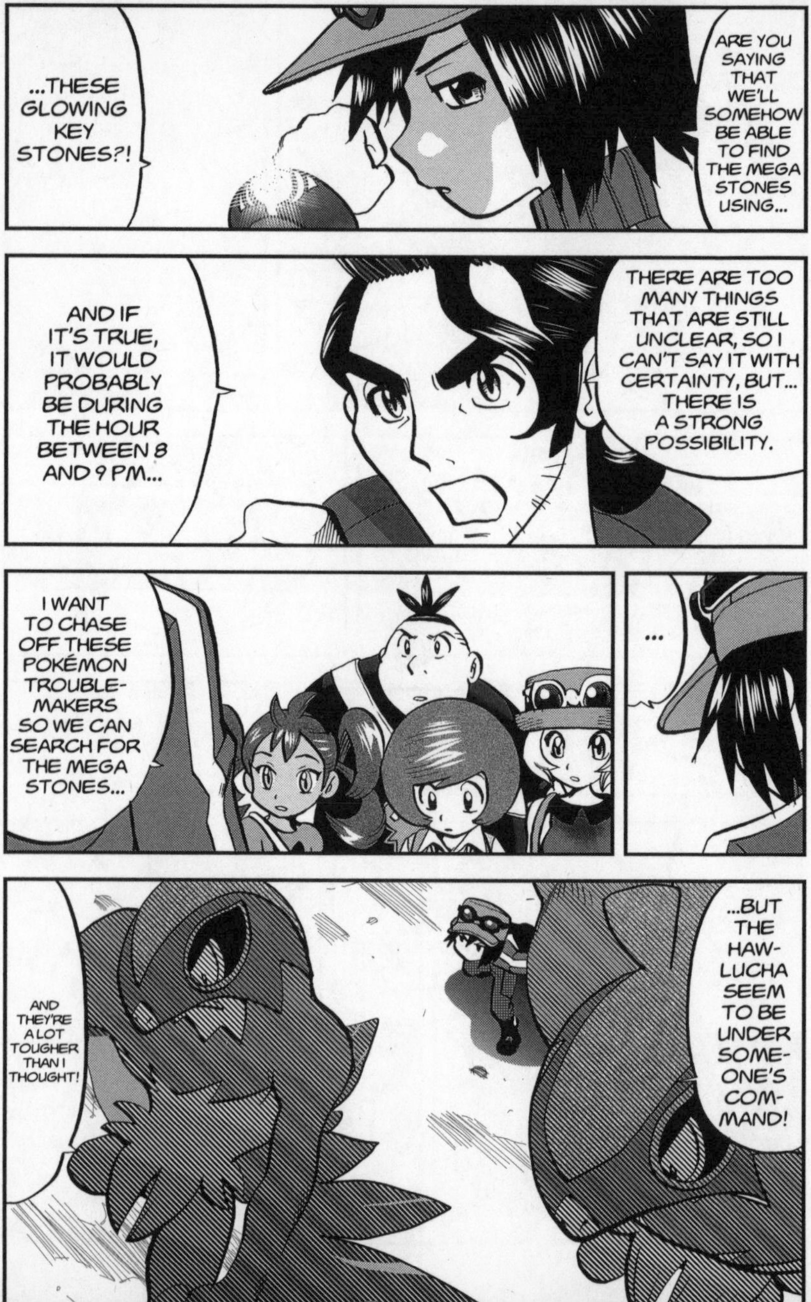
ARE YOU SAYING THAT WE'LL SOMEHOW BE ABLE TO FIND THE MEGA STONES USING...
...THESE GLOWING KEY STONES?!
THERE ARE TOO MANY THINGS THAT ARE STILL UNCLEAR, SO I CAN'T SAY IT WITH CERTAINTY, BUT... THERE IS A STRONG POSSIBILITY.
AND IF IT'S TRUE, IT WOULD PROBABLY BE DURING THE HOUR BETWEEN 8 AND 9 PM...
...
I WANT TO CHASE OFF THESE POKÉMON TROUBLE-MAKERS SO WE CAN SEARCH FOR THE MEGA STONES...
...BUT THE HAW-LUCHA SEEM TO BE UNDER SOME-ONE'S COM-MAND!
AND THEY'RE A LOT TOUGHER THAN I THOUGHT!

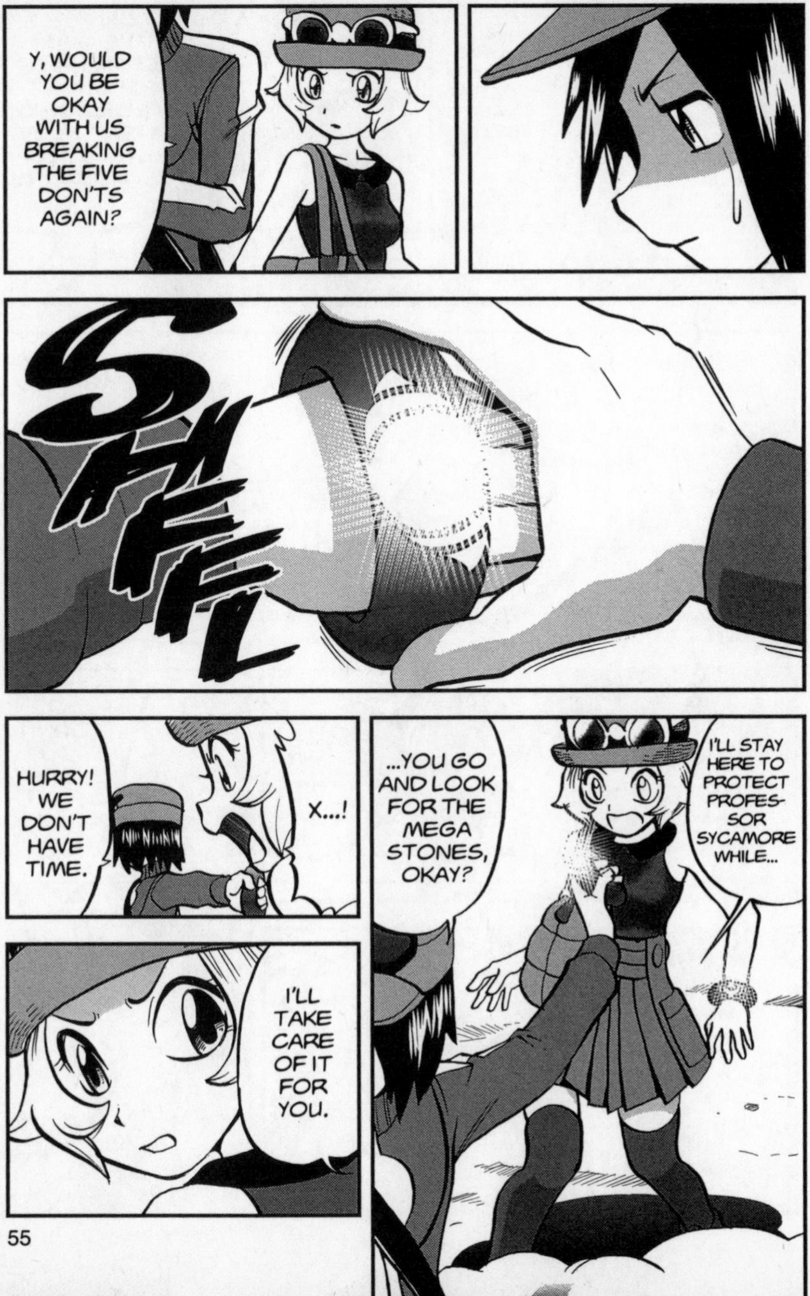
Y, WOULD YOU BE OKAY WITH US BREAKING THE FIVE DON'TS AGAIN?
SHFFL
I'LL STAY HERE TO PROTECT PROFES-SOR SYCAMORE WHILE...
...YOU GO AND LOOK FOR THE MEGA STONES, OKAY?
X...!
HURRY! WE DON'T HAVE TIME.
I'LL TAKE CARE OF IT FOR YOU.

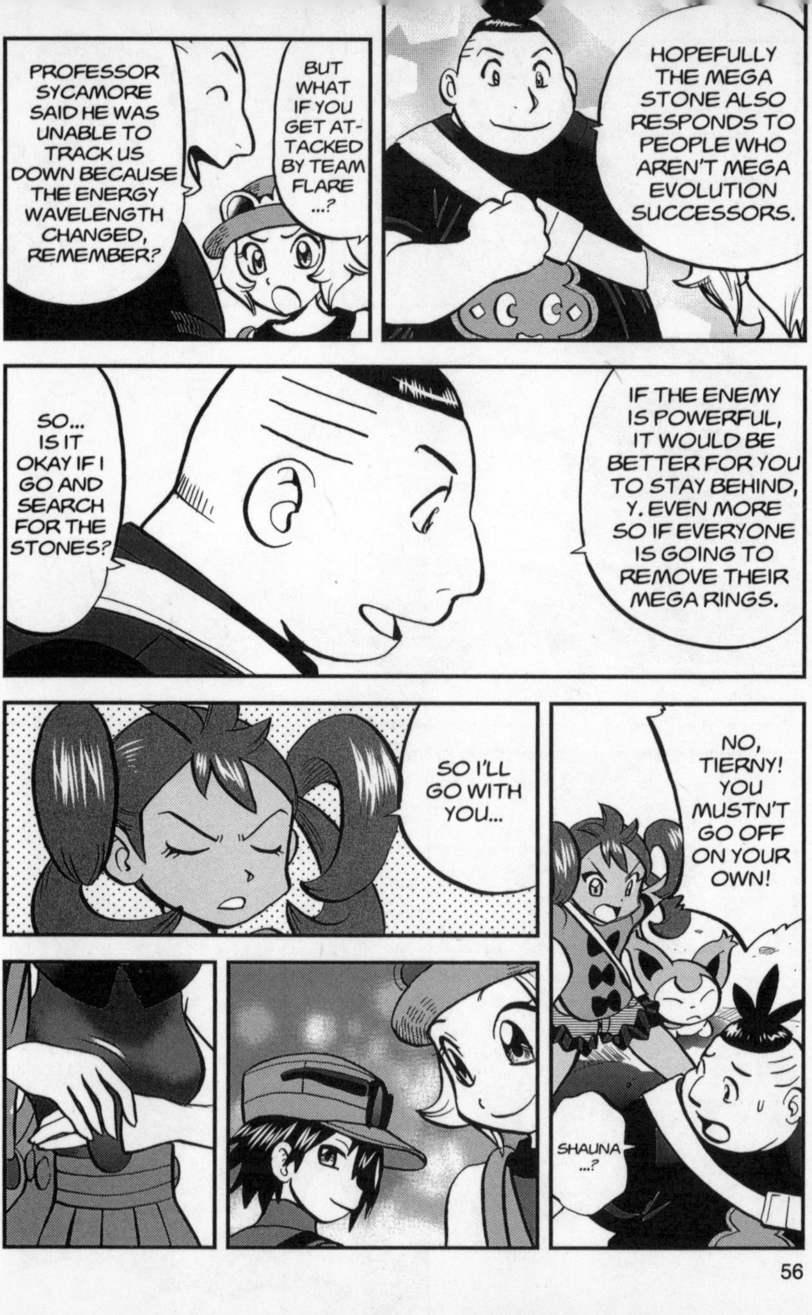
HOPEFULLY THE MEGA STONE ALSO RESPONDS TO PEOPLE WHO AREN'T MEGA EVOLUTION SUCCESSORS.
BUT WHAT IF YOU GET AT-TACKED BY TEAM FLARE ...?
PROFESSOR SYCAMORE SAID HE WAS UNABLE TO TRACK US DOWN BECAUSE THE ENERGY WAVELENGTH CHANGED, REMEMBER?
IF THE ENEMY IS POWERFUL, IT WOULD BE BETTER FOR YOU TO STAY BEHIND, Y. EVEN MORE SO IF EVERYONE IS GOING TO REMOVE THEIR MEGA RINGS.
SO... IS IT OKAY IF I GO AND SEARCH FOR THE STONES?
NO, TIERNY! YOU MUSTN'T GO OFF ON YOUR OWN!
SHAUNA ...?
SO I'LL GO WITH YOU...

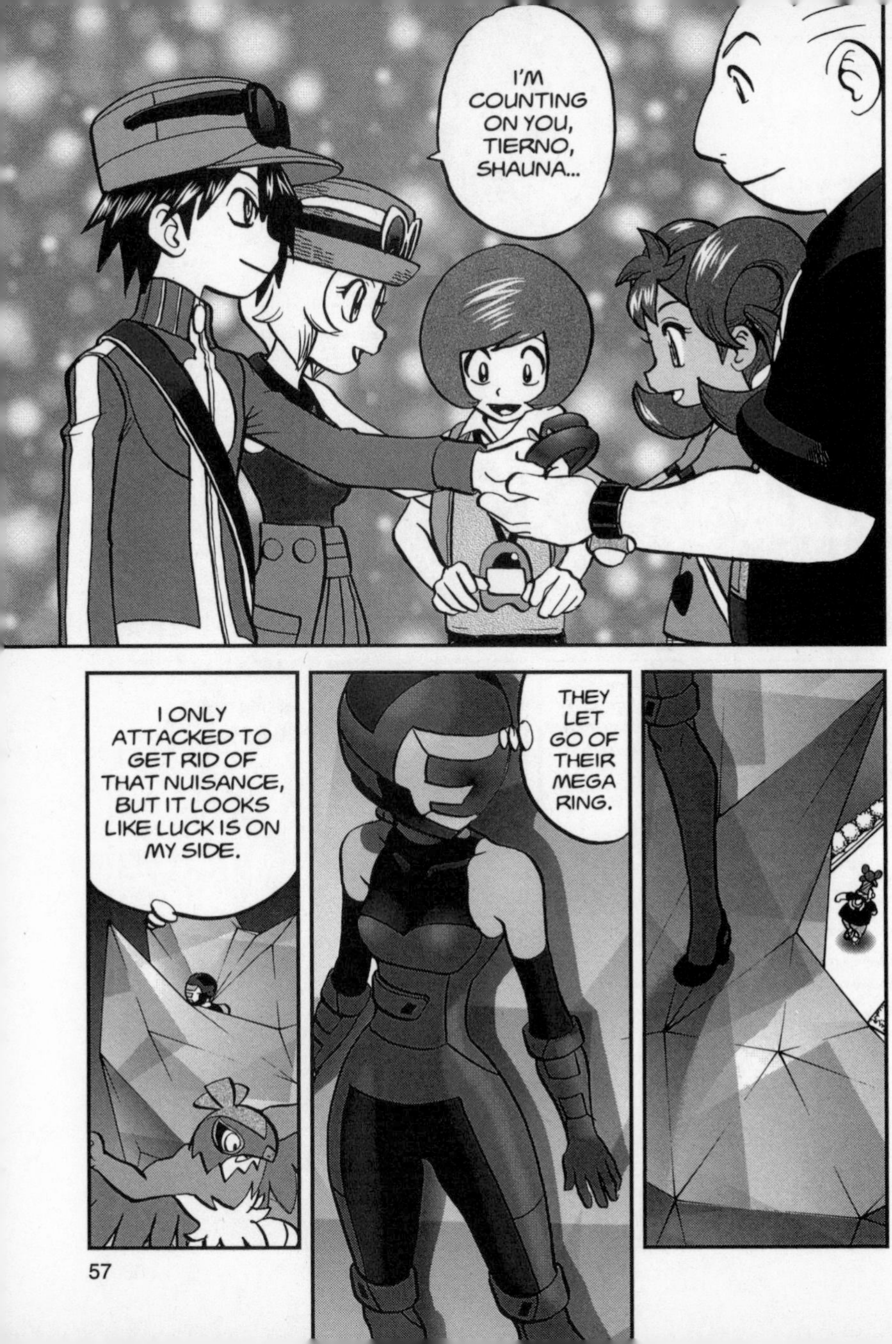
I'M COUNTING ON YOU, TIERNO, SHAUNA...
THEY LET GO OF THEIR MEGA RING.
I ONLY ATTACKED TO GET RID OF THAT NUISANCE, BUT IT LOOKS LIKE LUCK IS ON MY SIDE.

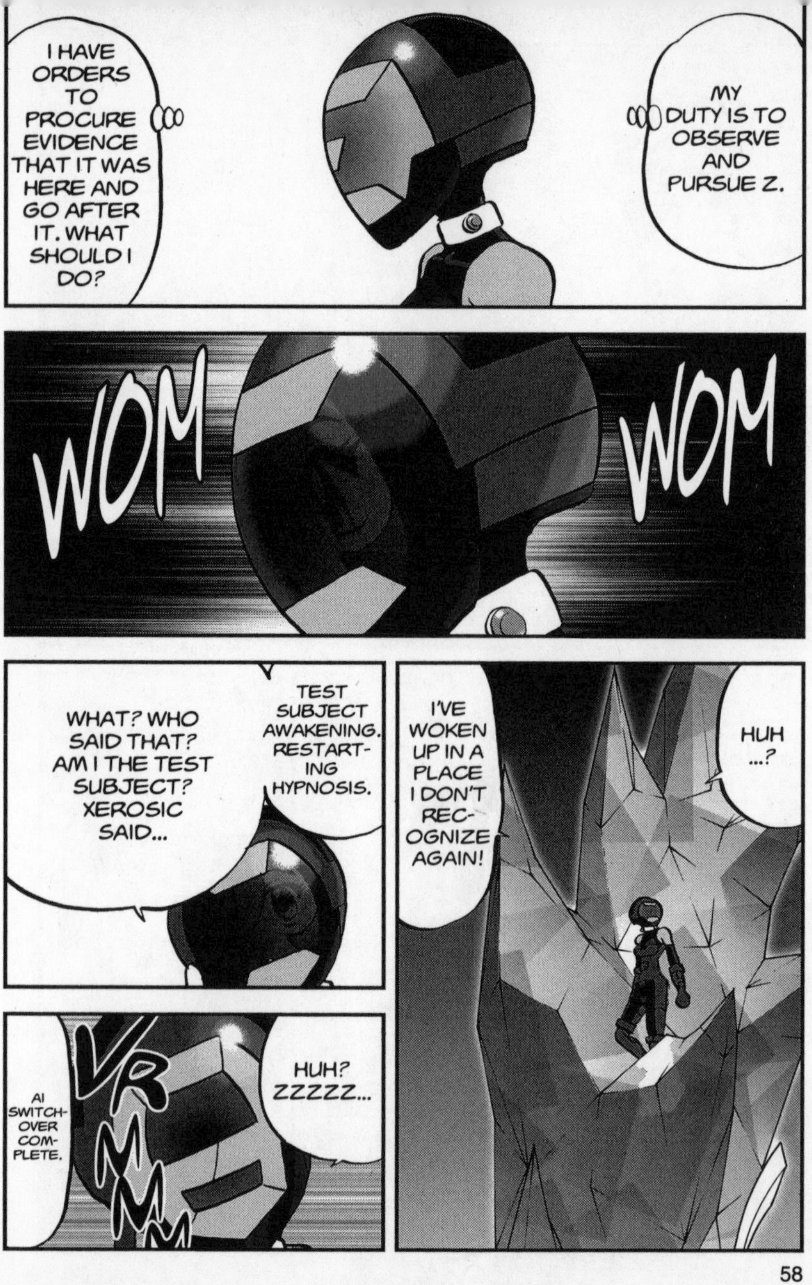
MY DUTY IS TO OBSERVE AND PURSUE Z.
I HAVE ORDERS TO PROCURE EVIDENCE THAT IT WAS HERE AND GO AFTER IT. WHAT SHOULD I DO?
WOM
WOM
HUH ...?
I'VE WOKEN UP IN A PLACE I DON'T REC-OGNIZE AGAIN!
TEST SUBJECT AWAKENING. RESTART-ING HYPNOSIS.
WHAT? WHO SAID THAT? AM I THE TEST SUBJECT? XEROSIC SAID...
HUH? ZZZZZ...
VRMMMM
AI SWITCH-OVER COM-PLETE.

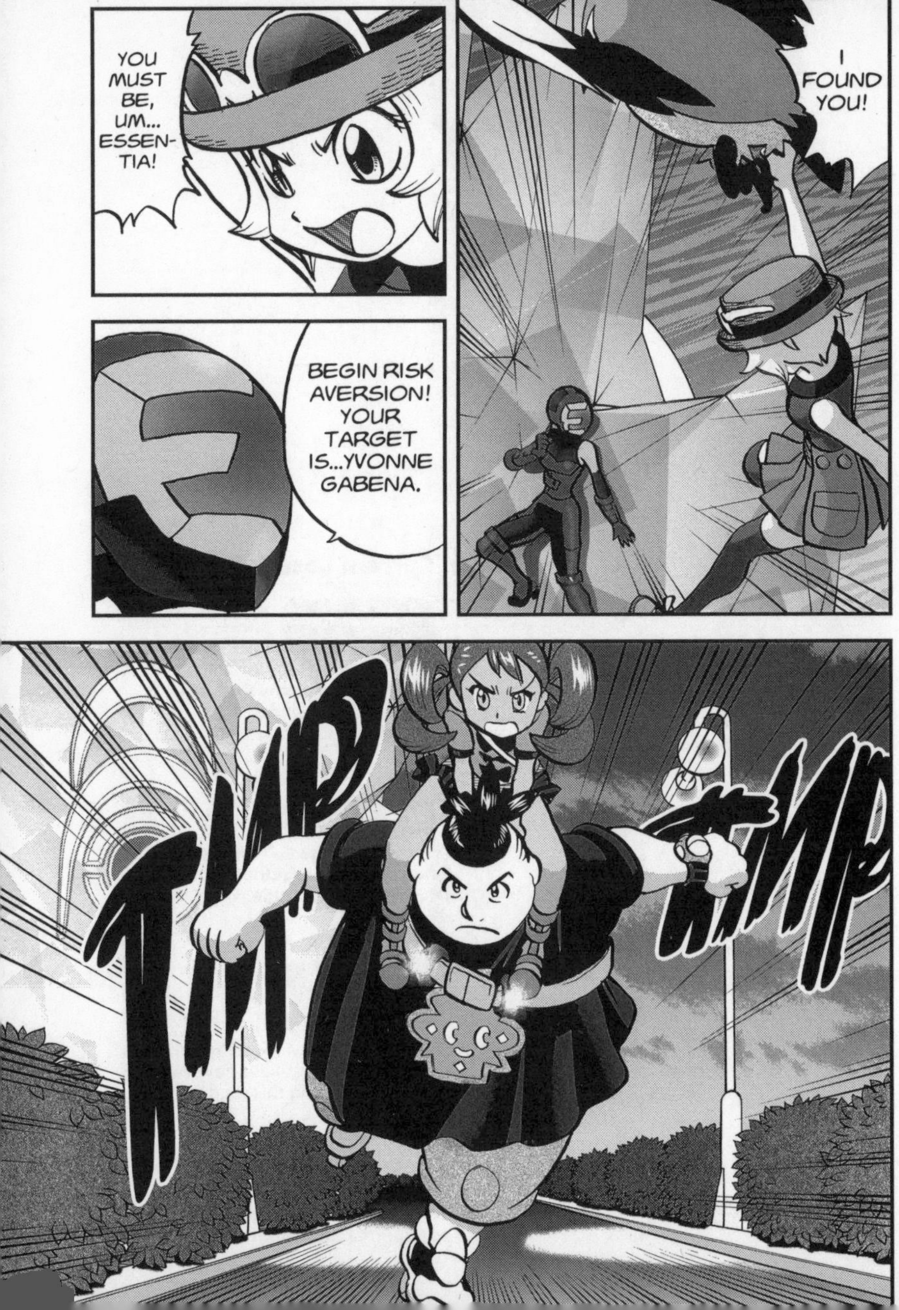
I FOUND YOU!
YOU MUST BE, UM... ESSENTIA!
BEGIN RISK AVERSION! YOUR TARGET IS...YVONNE GABENA.
THMP
THMP

Current Location

Route 15
Brun Way

This path has become a popular hangout for the wild and directionless kids of Lumiose City.

▼

Dendemille Town

A rural town where Pokémon and windmills work together to farm the land in a chilly latitude.

▼

Route 17
Mamoswine Road

Due to constant snowstorms and heavy snowfall, humans have no hope of traversing this road on foot.

▼

Anistar City

Some say the enigmatic device used as a sundial came from outer space.

Adventure 30 Pinsir Changes

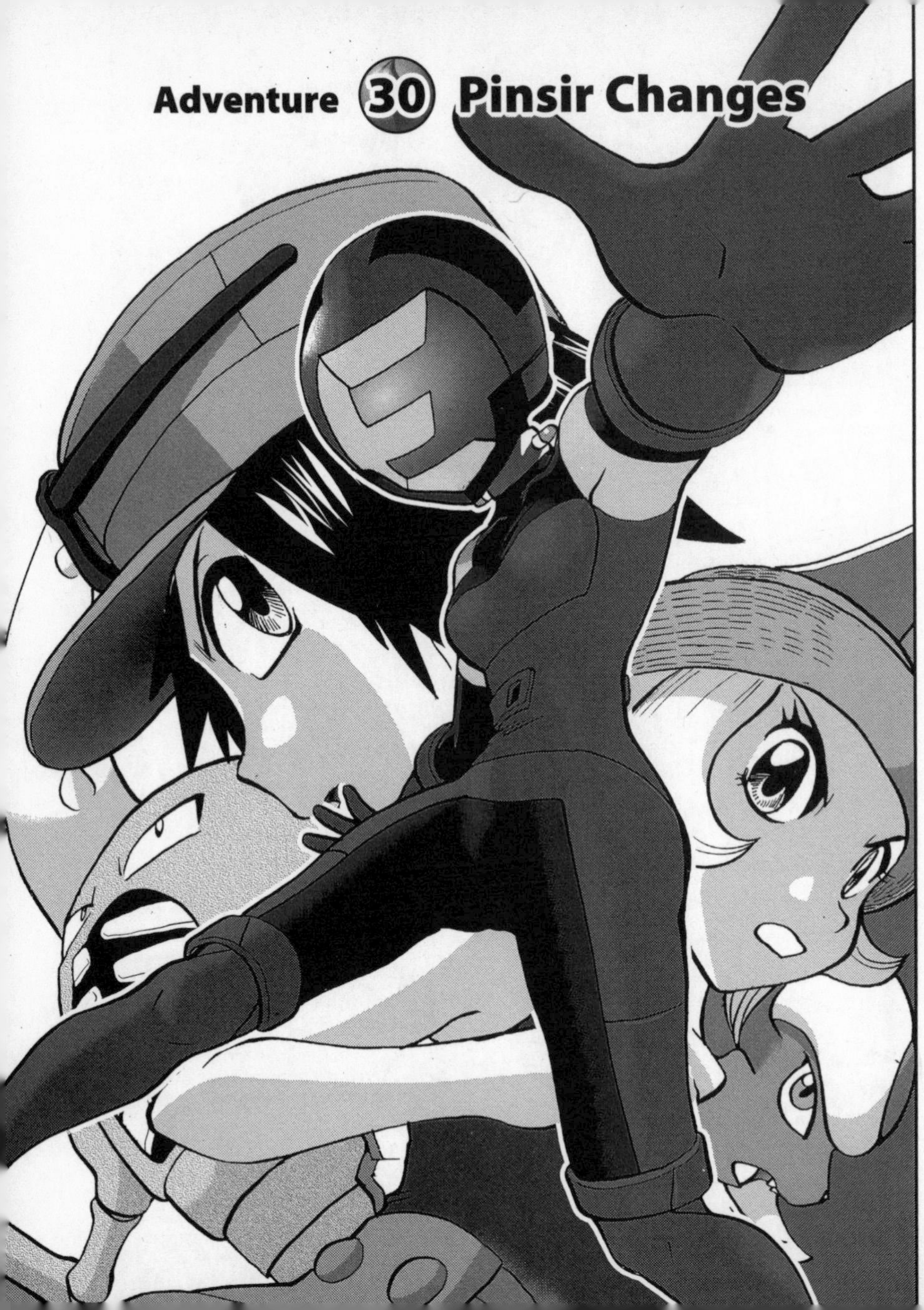

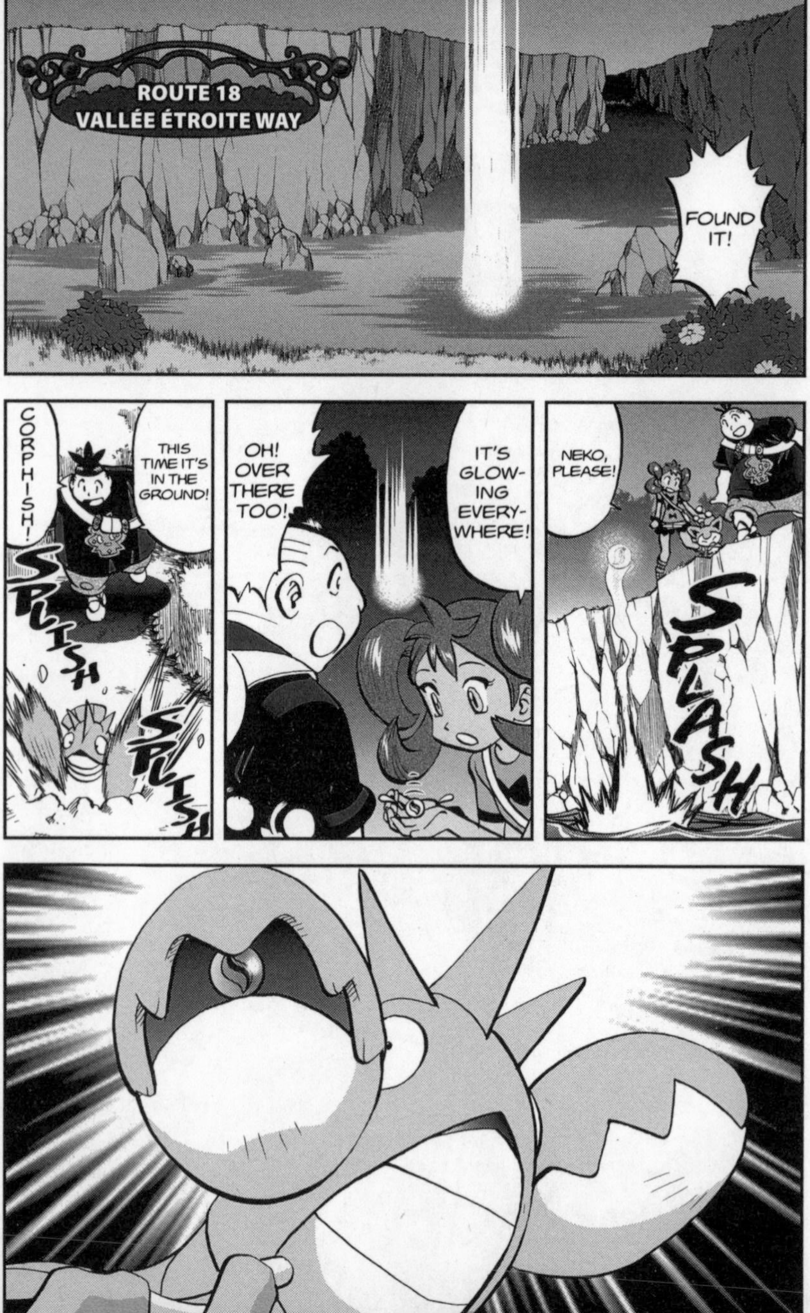
ROUTE 18 VALLÉE ÉTROITE WAY
FOUND IT!
NEKO, PLEASE!
SPLASH
IT'S GLOWING EVERYWHERE!
OH! OVER THERE TOO!
THIS TIME IT'S IN THE GROUND!
CORPHISH!
SPLISH
SPLISH

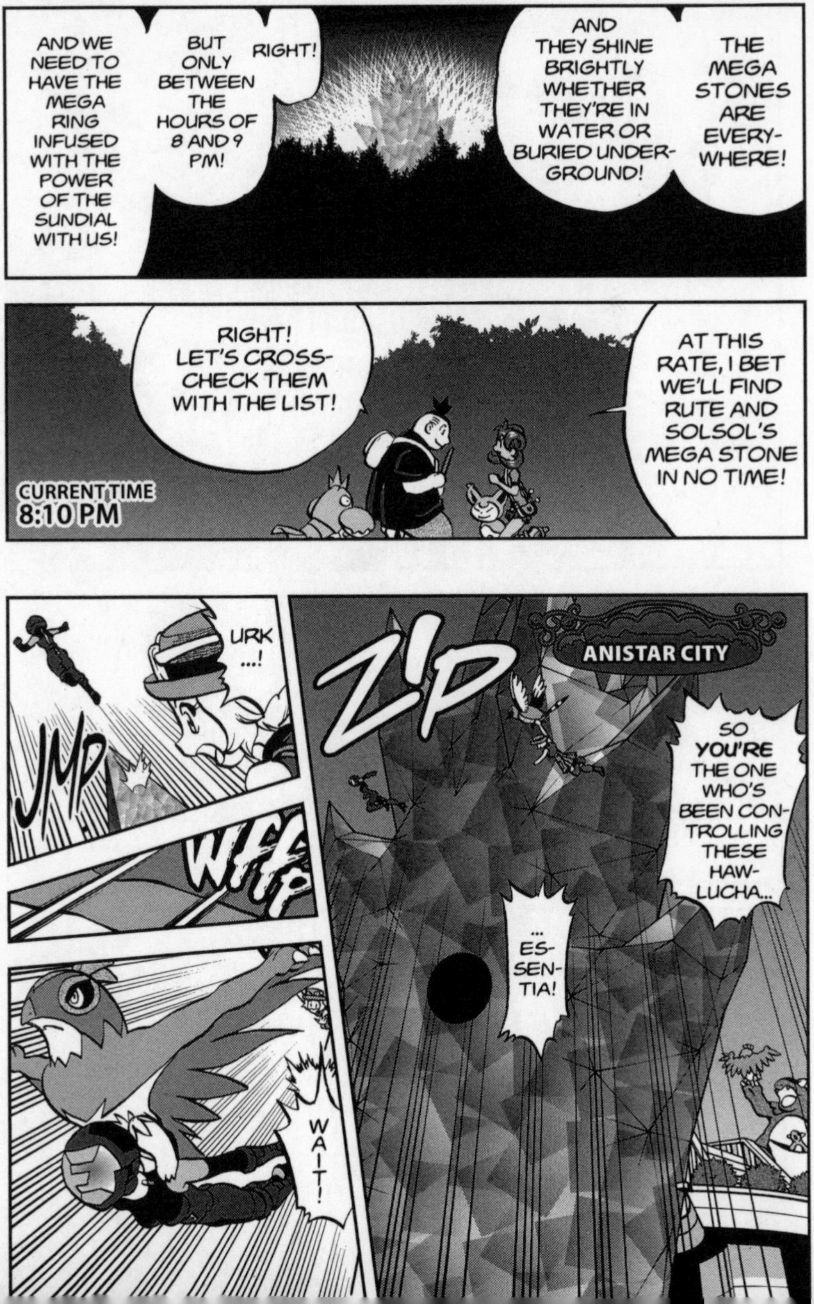
THE MEGA STONES ARE EVERY-WHERE!
AND THEY SHINE BRIGHTLY WHETHER THEY'RE IN WATER OR BURIED UNDER-GROUND!
RIGHT!
BUT ONLY BETWEEN THE HOURS OF 8 AND 9 PM!
AND WE NEED TO HAVE THE MEGA RING INFUSED WITH THE POWER OF THE SUNDIAL WITH US!
AT THIS RATE, I BET WE'LL FIND RUTE AND SOLSOL'S MEGA STONE IN NO TIME!
RIGHT! LET'S CROSS-CHECK THEM WITH THE LIST!
CURRENT TIME 8:10 PM
ANISTAR CITY
ZIP
SO **YOU'RE** THE ONE WHO'S BEEN CON-TROLLING THESE HAW-LUCHA...
... ES-SEN-TIA!
URK ...!
JMP
WFFP
WAIT!

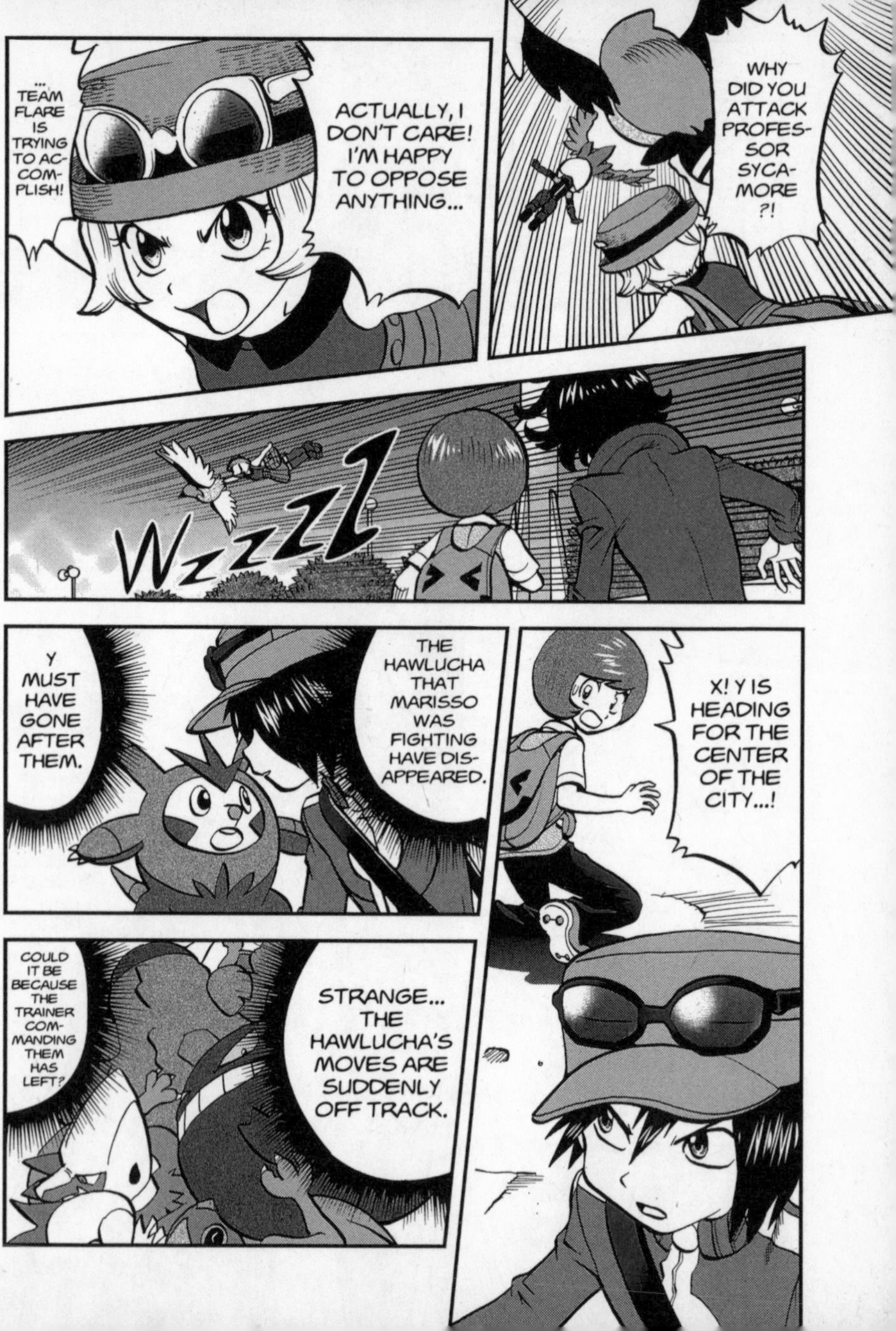
WHY DID YOU ATTACK PROFESSOR SYCAMORE?!
ACTUALLY, I DON'T CARE! I'M HAPPY TO OPPOSE ANYTHING...
...TEAM FLARE IS TRYING TO ACCOMPLISH!
WZZZZ
X! Y IS HEADING FOR THE CENTER OF THE CITY...!
THE HAWLUCHA THAT MARISSO WAS FIGHTING HAVE DISAPPEARED.
Y MUST HAVE GONE AFTER THEM.
STRANGE... THE HAWLUCHA'S MOVES ARE SUDDENLY OFF TRACK.
COULD IT BE BECAUSE THE TRAINER COMMANDING THEM HAS LEFT?

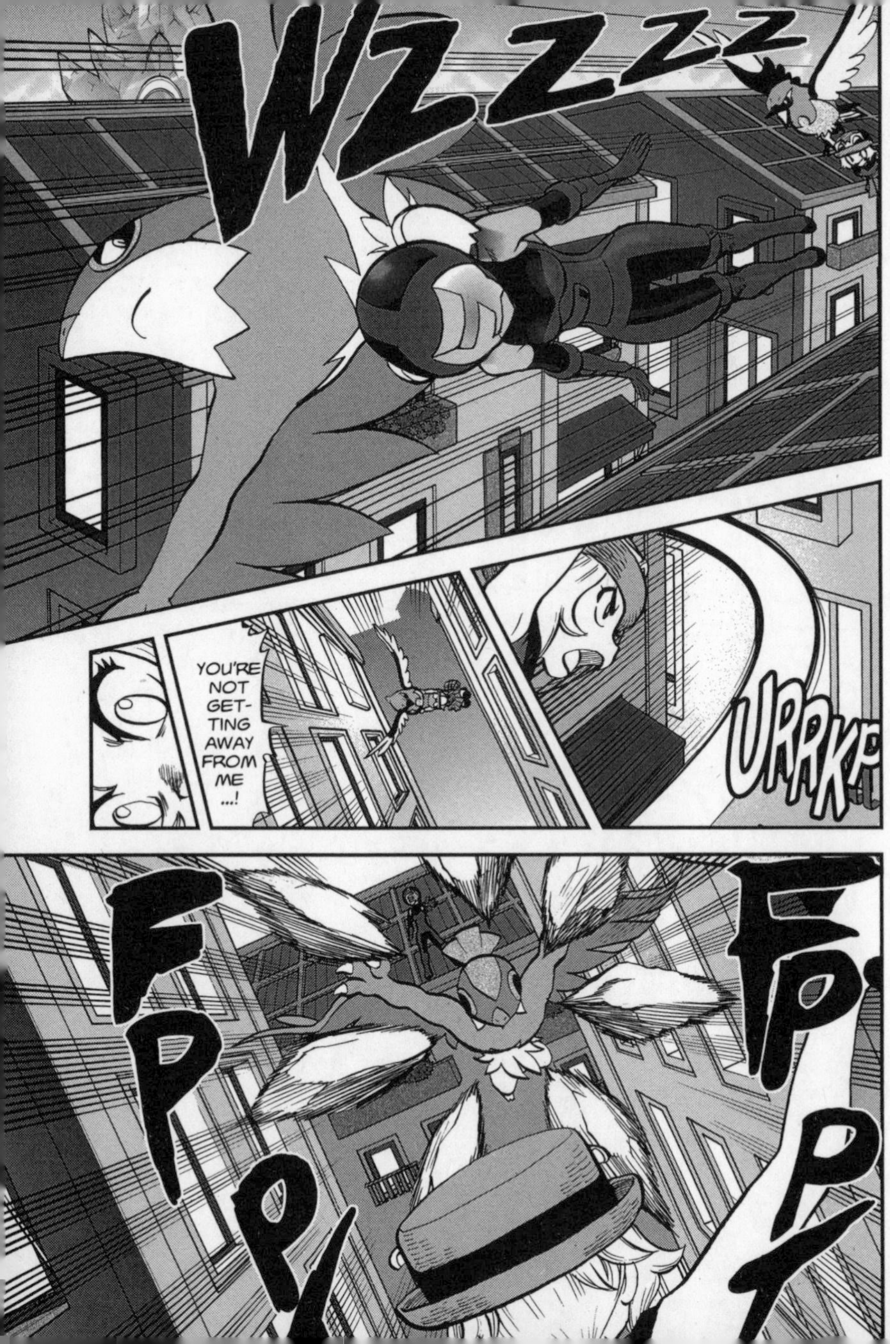
WIZZZZZ
URRK
YOU'RE NOT GETTING AWAY FROM ME ...!
FPPP
FPPP

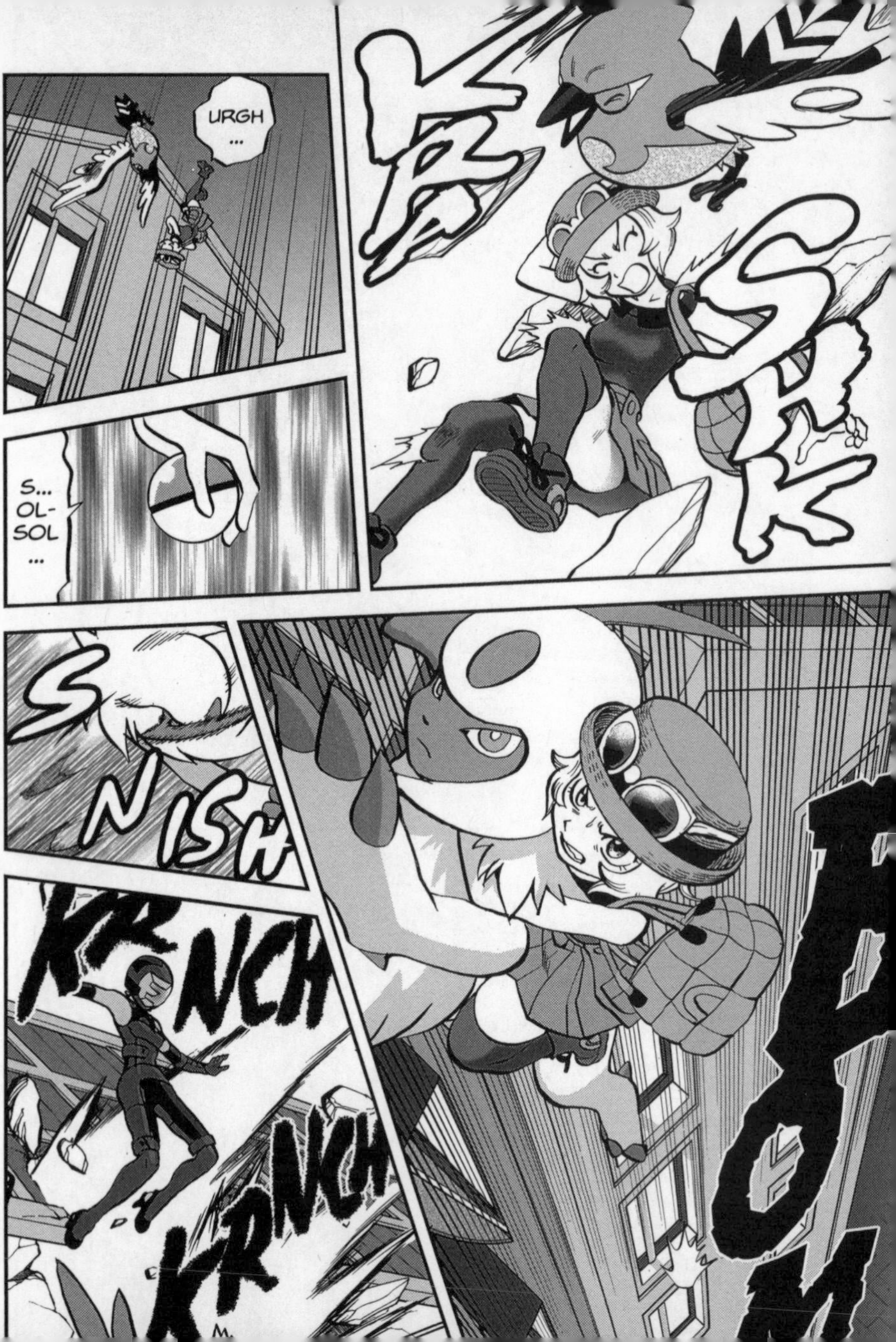
URGH ...
S... OL-SOL ...
SNISH
KRNCH
KRNCH

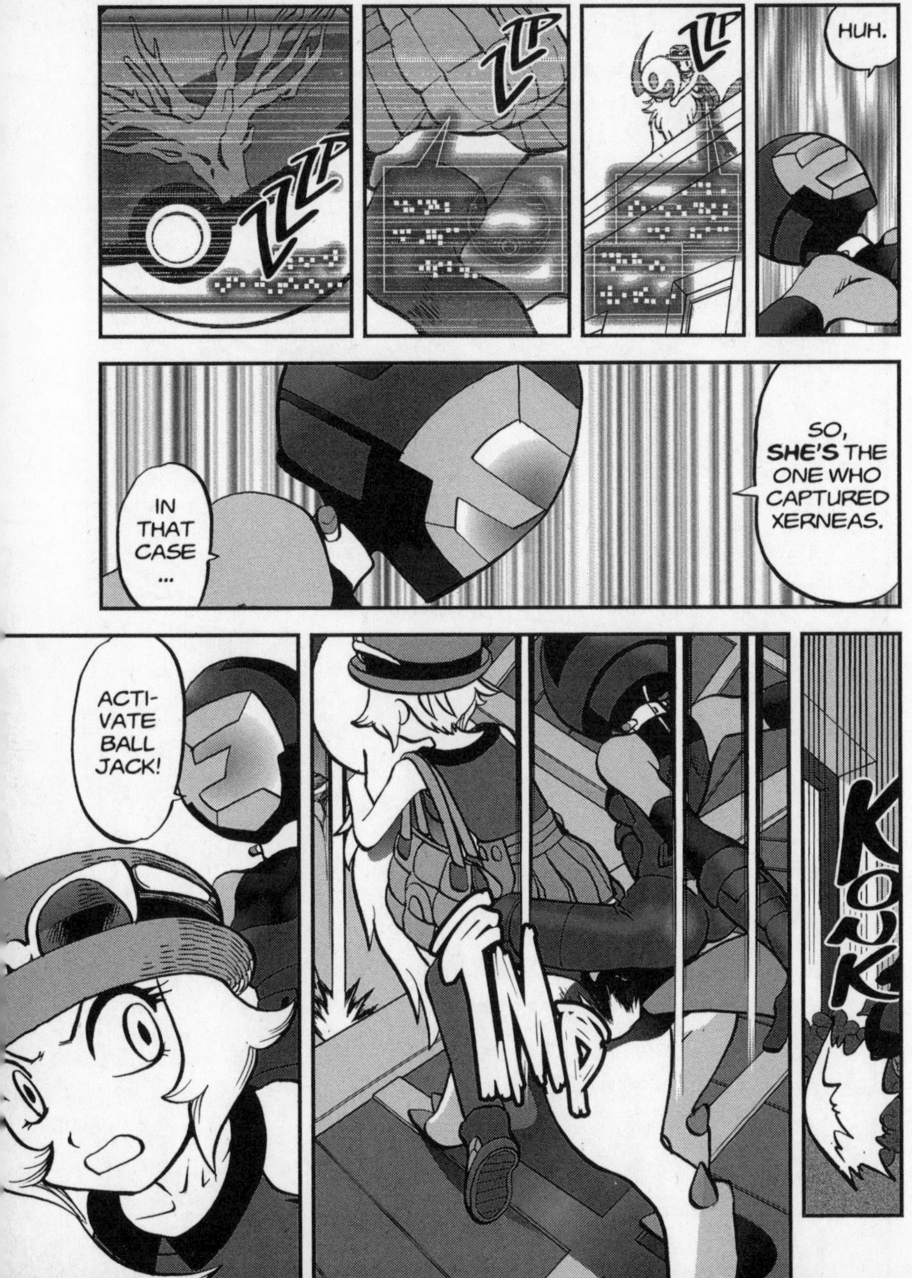
HUH.
ZZP
ZZP
ZZZP
SO, SHE'S THE ONE WHO CAPTURED XERNEAS.
IN THAT CASE ...
TMP
ACTI-VATE BALL JACK!

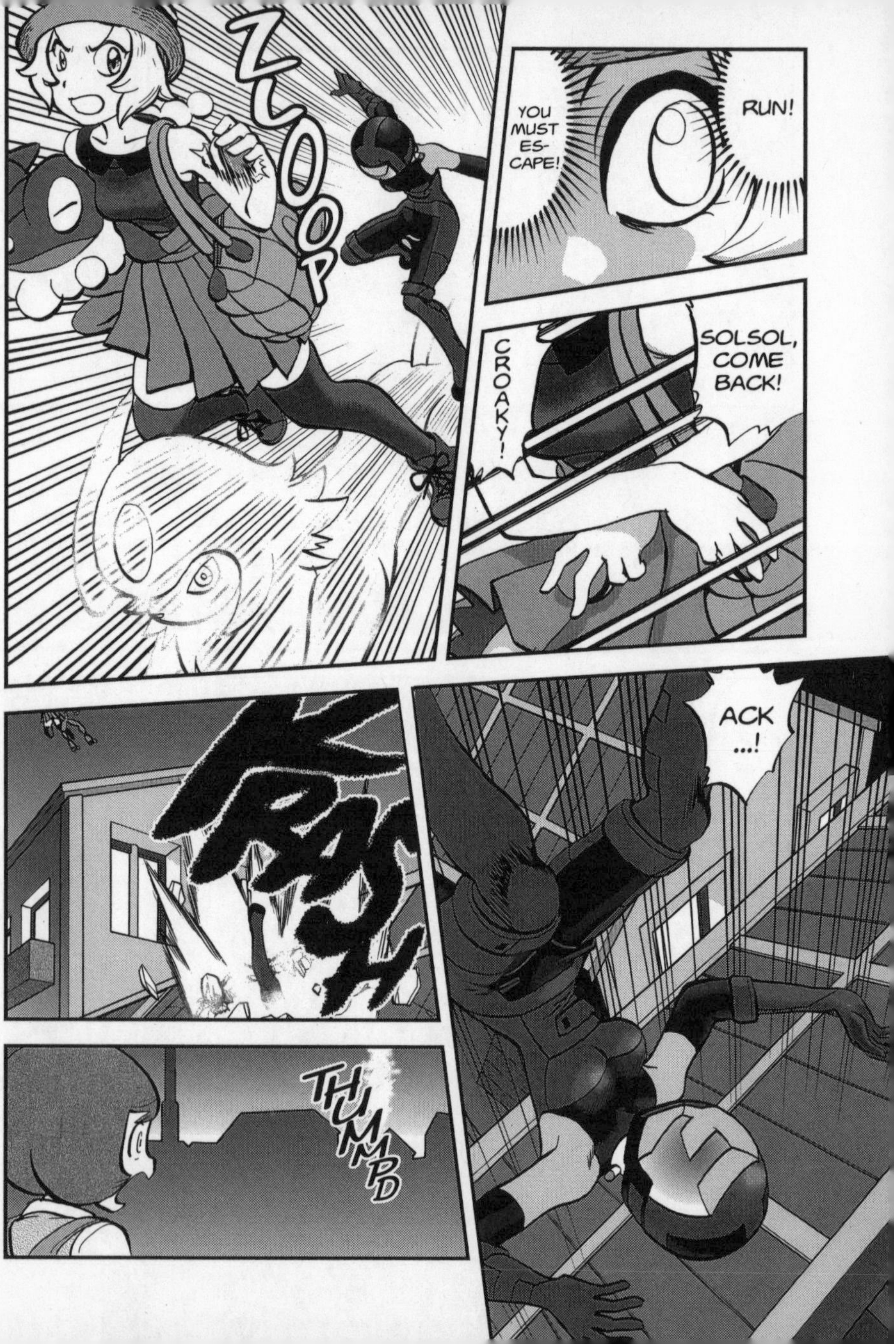
RUN!
YOU MUST ES-CAPE!
SOLSOL, COME BACK!
CROAKY!
ZLOOOP
ACK ...!
KRASH
THUMMPD

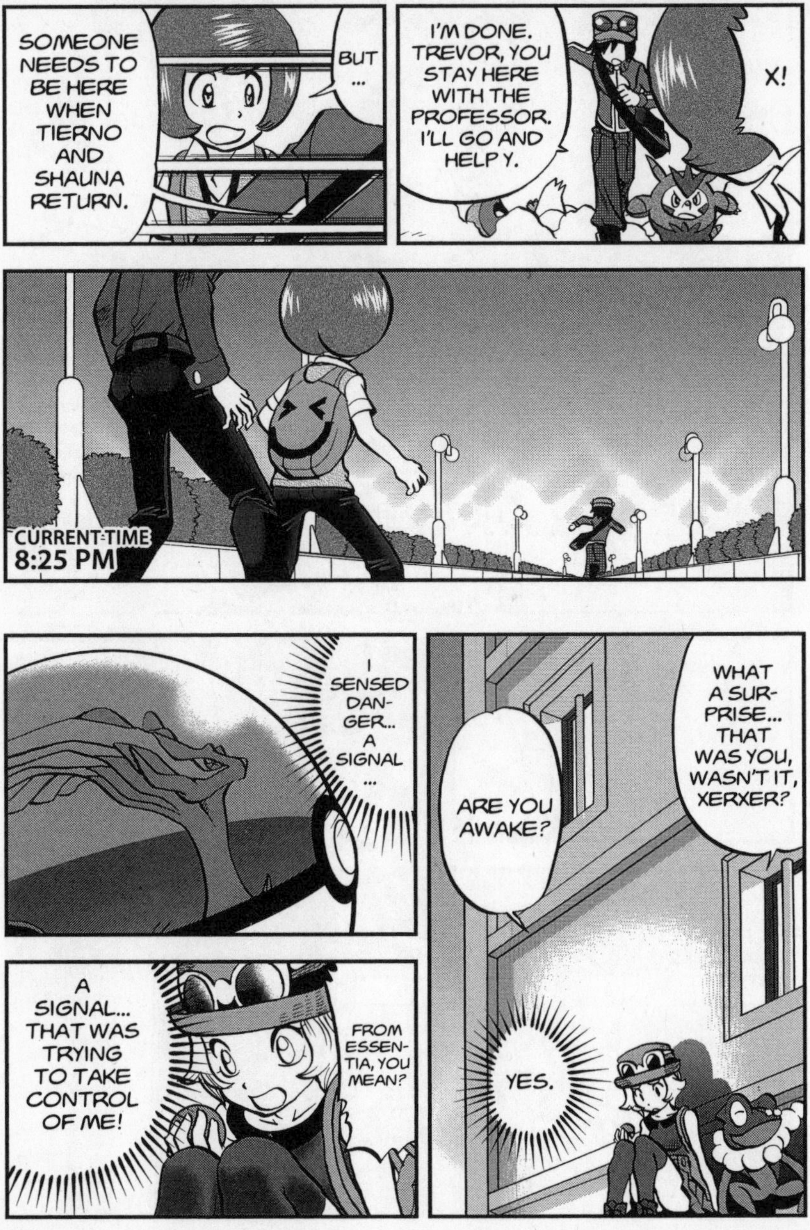

I'M DONE. TREVOR, YOU STAY HERE WITH THE PROFESSOR. I'LL GO AND HELP Y.
X!
BUT ...
SOMEONE NEEDS TO BE HERE WHEN TIERNO AND SHAUNA RETURN.
CURRENT TIME
8:25 PM
WHAT A SUR-PRISE... THAT WAS YOU, WASN'T IT, XERXER?
ARE YOU AWAKE?
YES.
I SENSED DAN-GER... A SIGNAL ...
FROM ESSEN-TIA, YOU MEAN?
A SIGNAL... THAT WAS TRYING TO TAKE CONTROL OF ME!

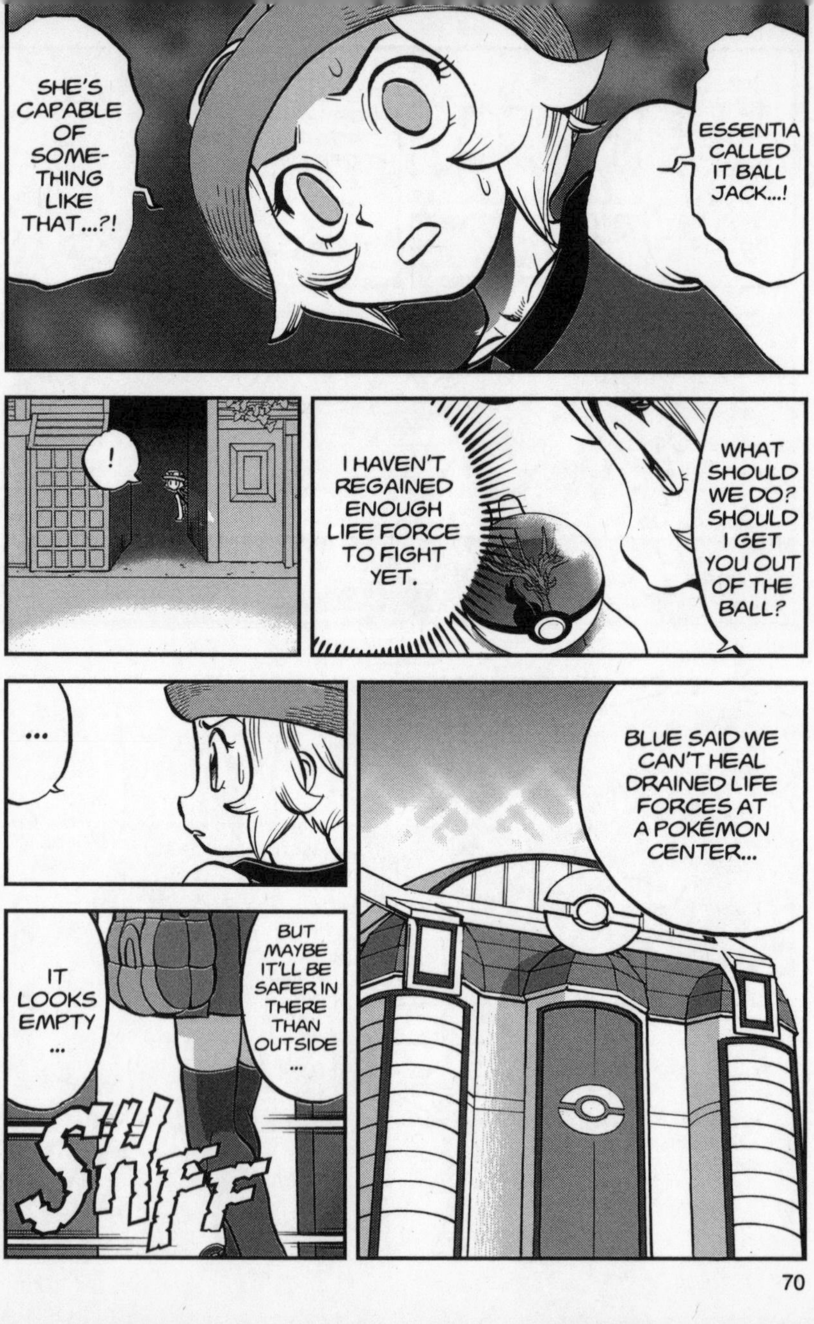
ESSENTIA CALLED IT BALL JACK...!
SHE'S CAPABLE OF SOME-THING LIKE THAT...?!
WHAT SHOULD WE DO? SHOULD I GET YOU OUT OF THE BALL?
I HAVEN'T REGAINED ENOUGH LIFE FORCE TO FIGHT YET.
!
BLUE SAID WE CAN'T HEAL DRAINED LIFE FORCES AT A POKÉMON CENTER...
...
BUT MAYBE IT'LL BE SAFER IN THERE THAN OUTSIDE...
IT LOOKS EMPTY...
SHFF

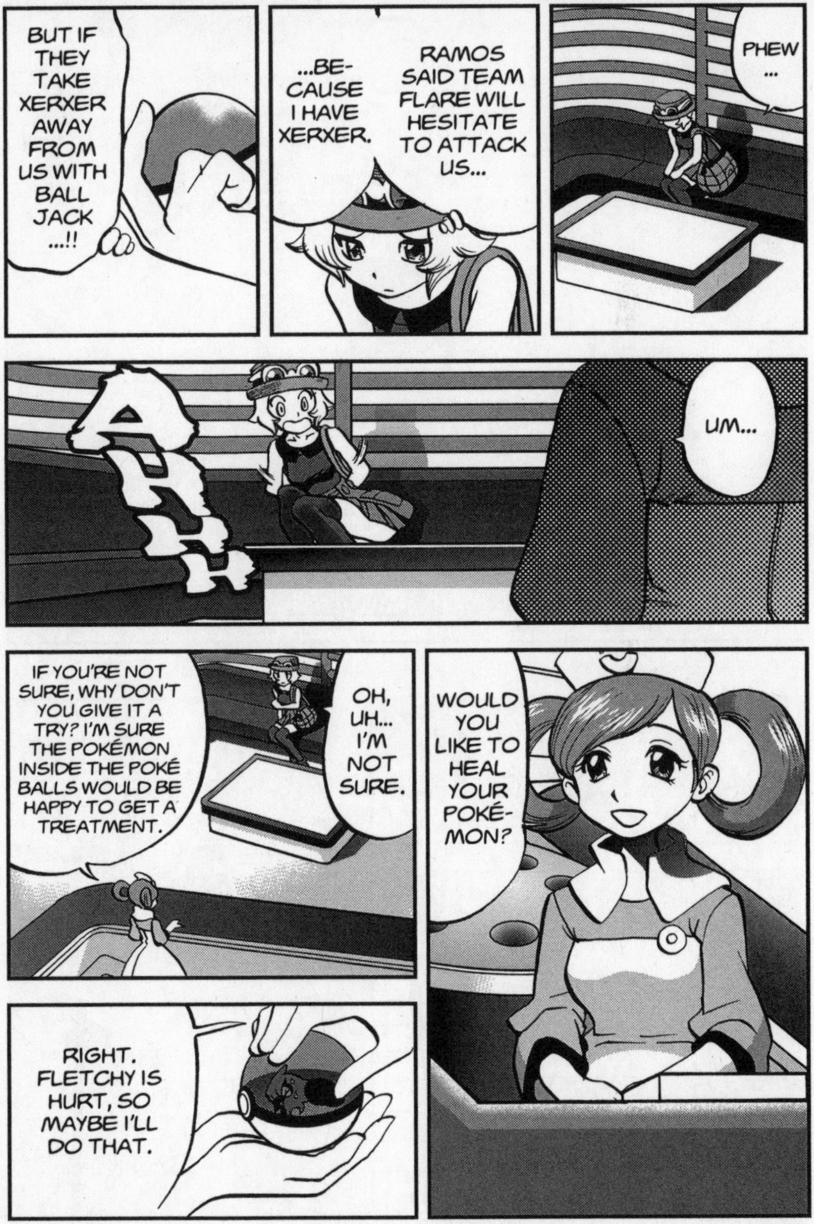

PHEW ...
RAMOS SAID TEAM FLARE WILL HESITATE TO ATTACK US...
...BE- CAUSE I HAVE XERXER.
BUT IF THEY TAKE XERXER AWAY FROM US WITH BALL JACK ...!!
UM...
AHHH
WOULD YOU LIKE TO HEAL YOUR POKÉ- MON?
OH, UH... I'M NOT SURE.
IF YOU'RE NOT SURE, WHY DON'T YOU GIVE IT A TRY? I'M SURE THE POKÉMON INSIDE THE POKÉ BALLS WOULD BE HAPPY TO GET A TREATMENT.
RIGHT. FLETCHY IS HURT, SO MAYBE I'LL DO THAT.

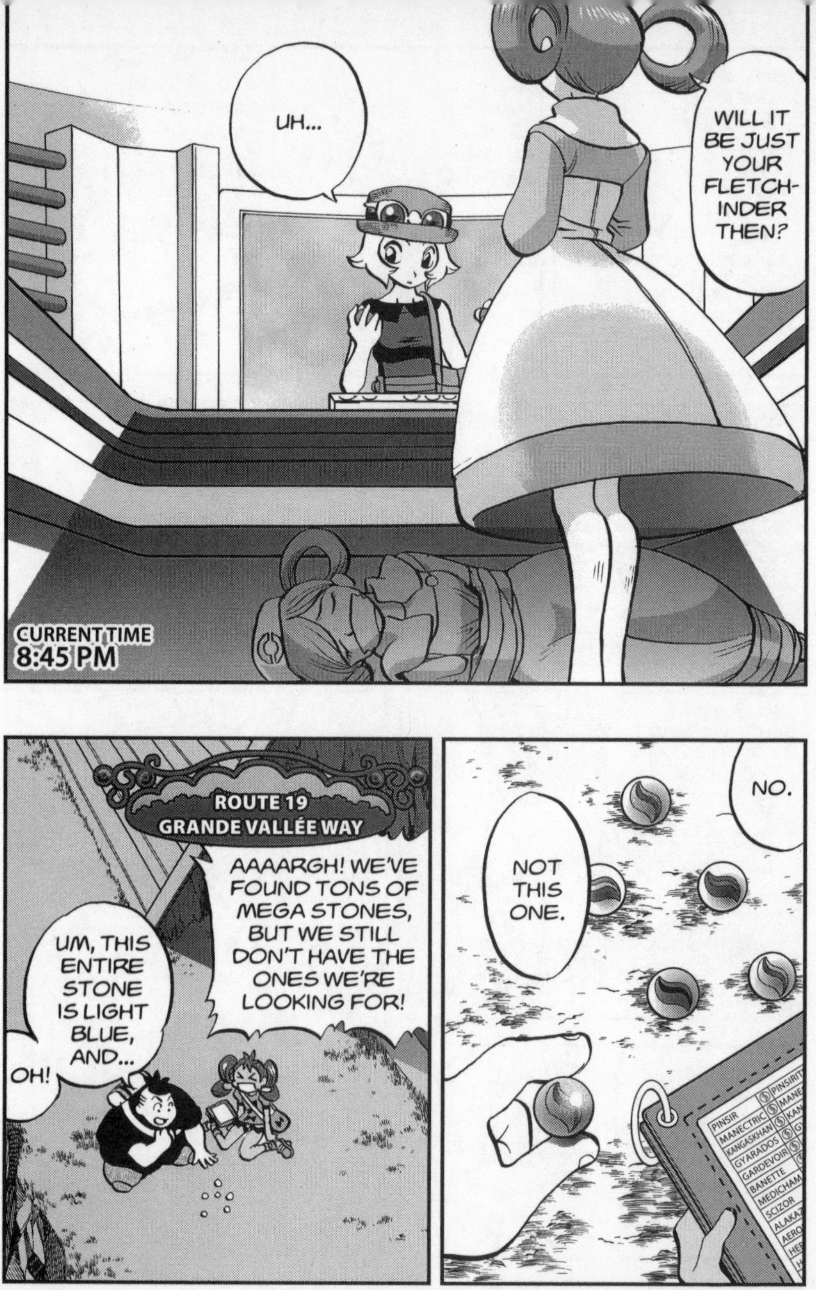
WILL IT BE JUST YOUR FLETCH-INDER THEN?
UH...
CURRENT TIME 8:45 PM
NO.
NOT THIS ONE.
PINSIR
MANECTRIC
KANGASKHAN
GYARADOS
GARDEVOIR
BANETTE
MEDICHAM
SCIZOR
ROUTE 19 GRANDE VALLÉE WAY
AAAARGH! WE'VE FOUND TONS OF MEGA STONES, BUT WE STILL DON'T HAVE THE ONES WE'RE LOOKING FOR!
UM, THIS ENTIRE STONE IS LIGHT BLUE, AND...
OH!

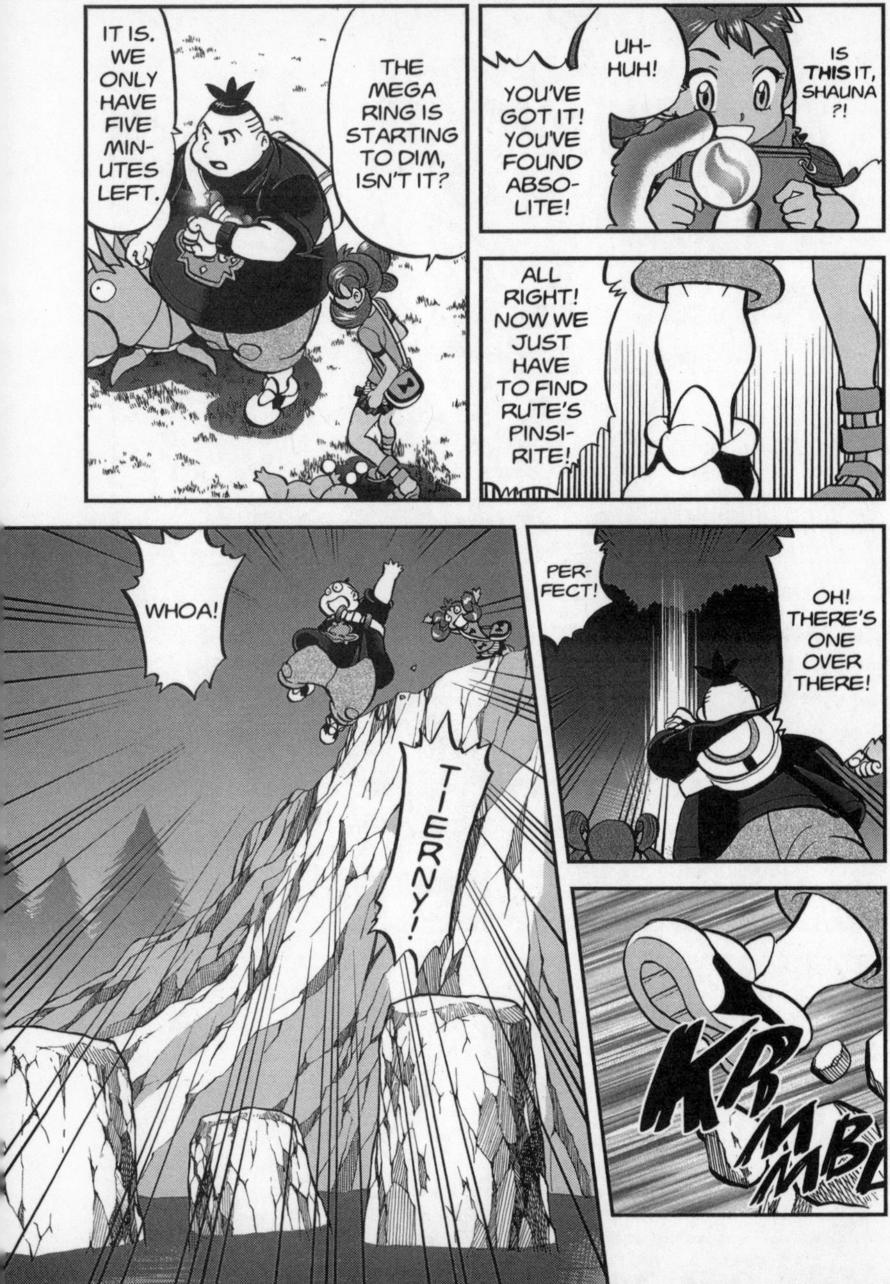
IS THIS IT, SHAUNA?!
UH-HUH!
YOU'VE GOT IT! YOU'VE FOUND ABSO-LITE!
ALL RIGHT! NOW WE JUST HAVE TO FIND RUTE'S PINSI-RITE!
THE MEGA RING IS STARTING TO DIM, ISN'T IT?
IT IS. WE ONLY HAVE FIVE MIN-UTES LEFT.
OH! THERE'S ONE OVER THERE!
PER-FECT!
KRMMBL
WHOA!
TIERNY!

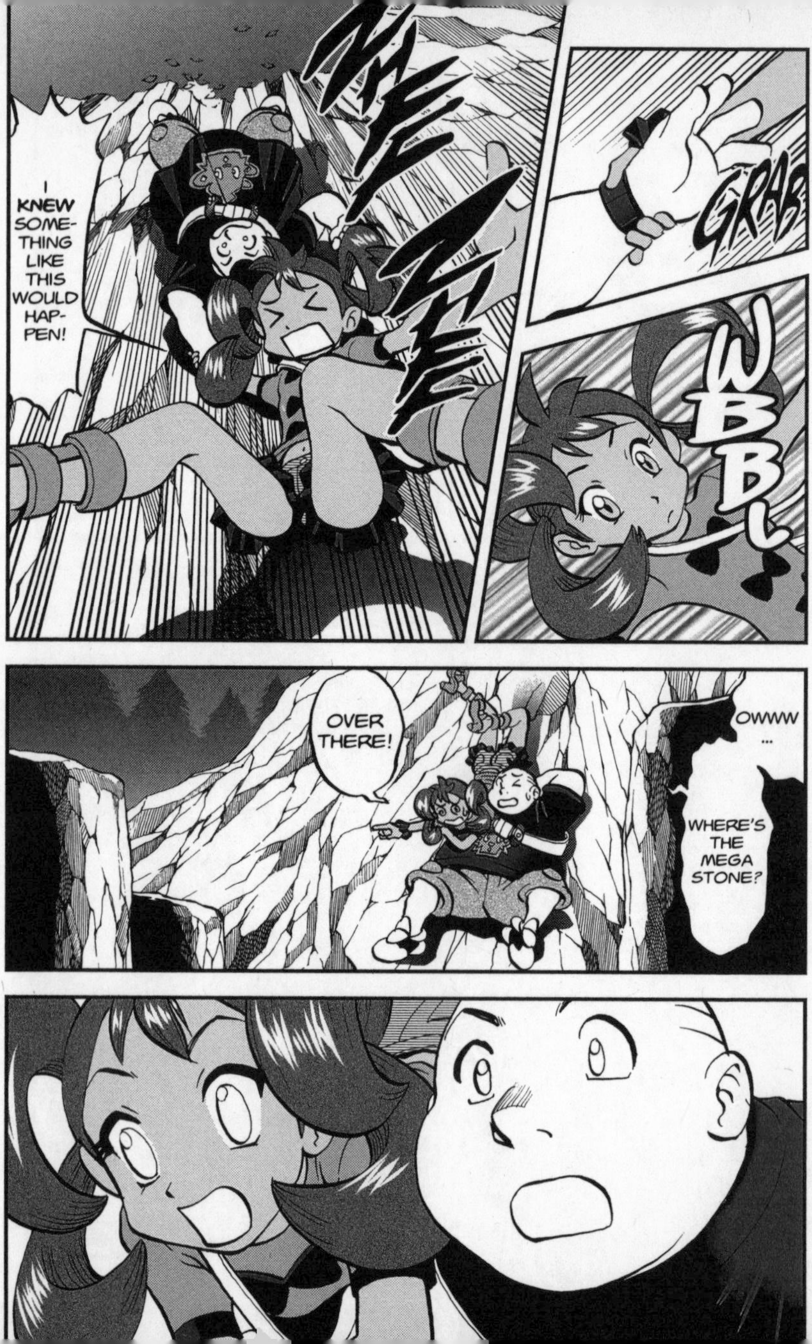
GRAB
WBBL
I KNEW SOMETHING LIKE THIS WOULD HAPPEN!
OWWW...
WHERE'S THE MEGA STONE?
OVER THERE!

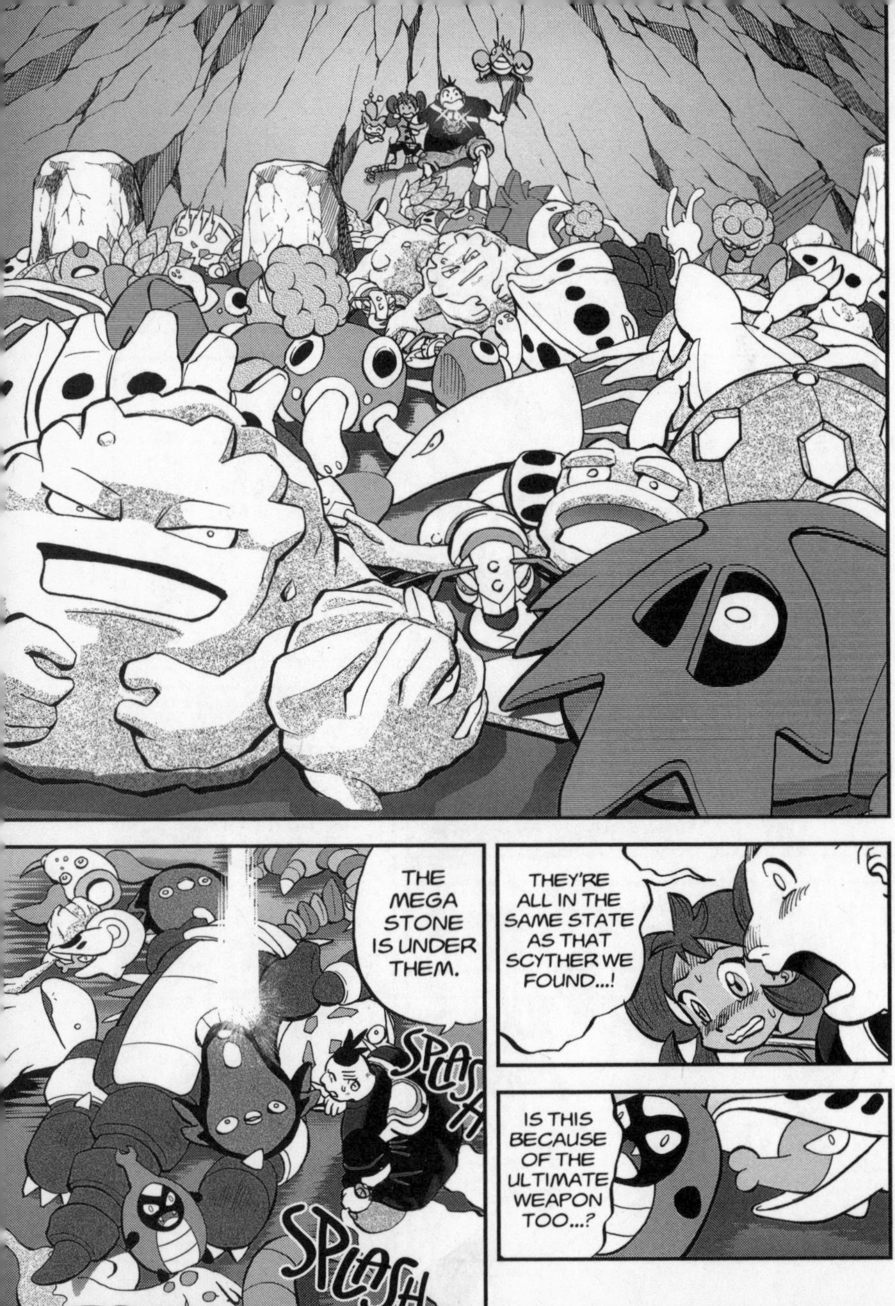
THEY'RE ALL IN THE SAME STATE AS THAT SCYTHER WE FOUND...!
IS THIS BECAUSE OF THE ULTIMATE WEAPON TOO...?
THE MEGA STONE IS UNDER THEM.
SPLASH
SPLASH

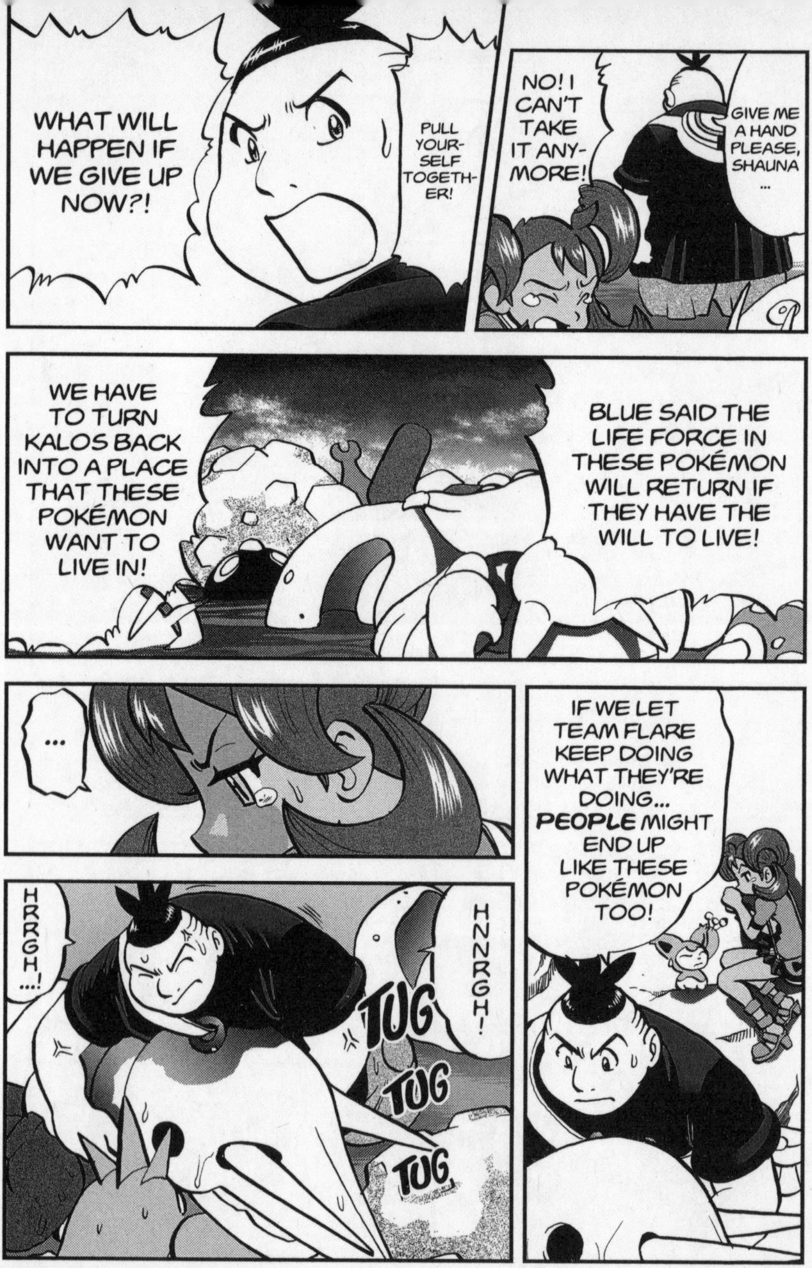
GIVE ME A HAND PLEASE, SHAUNA...
NO! I CAN'T TAKE IT ANYMORE!
PULL YOURSELF TOGETHER!
WHAT WILL HAPPEN IF WE GIVE UP NOW?!
BLUE SAID THE LIFE FORCE IN THESE POKÉMON WILL RETURN IF THEY HAVE THE WILL TO LIVE!
WE HAVE TO TURN KALOS BACK INTO A PLACE THAT THESE POKÉMON WANT TO LIVE IN!
IF WE LET TEAM FLARE KEEP DOING WHAT THEY'RE DOING... **PEOPLE** MIGHT END UP LIKE THESE POKÉMON TOO!
...
HNNRGH!
TUG
TUG
TUG
HRRGH...!

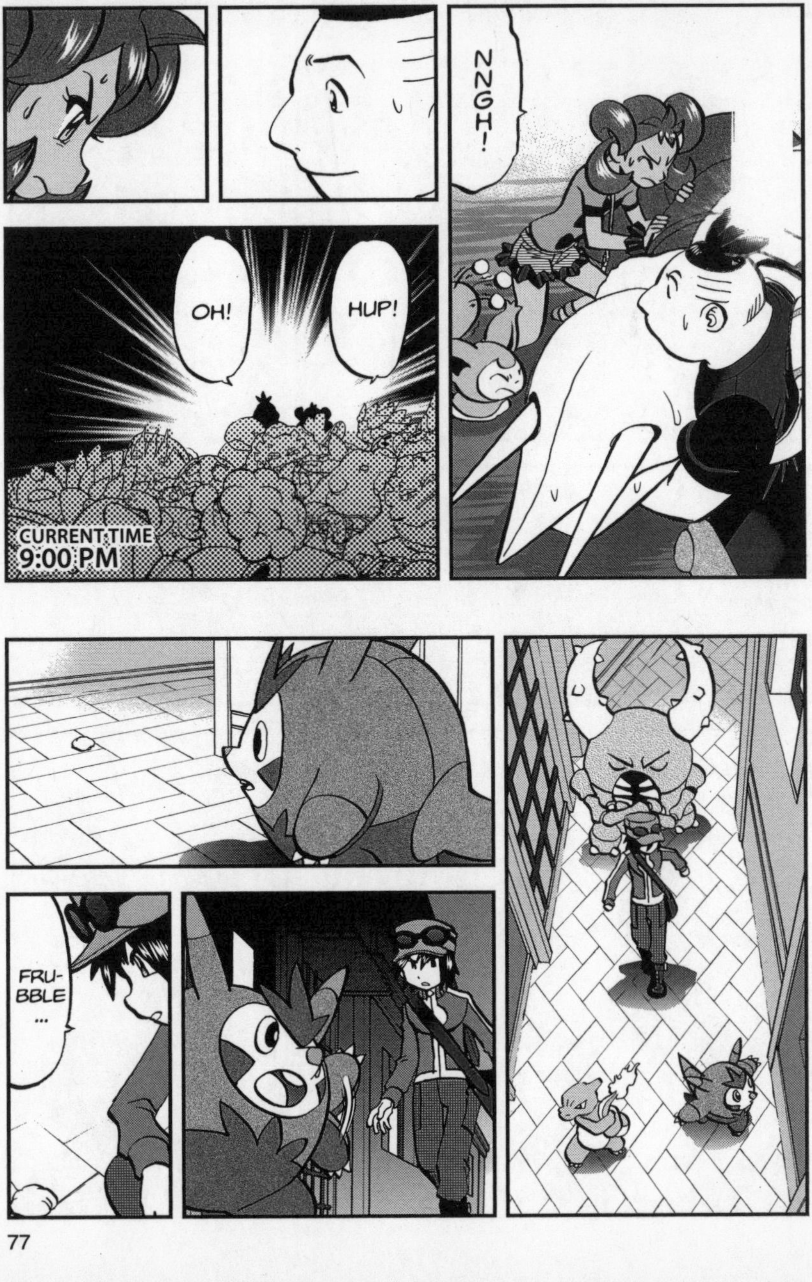
NNGH!
HUP!
OH!
CURRENT TIME 9:00 PM
FRU-BBLE...

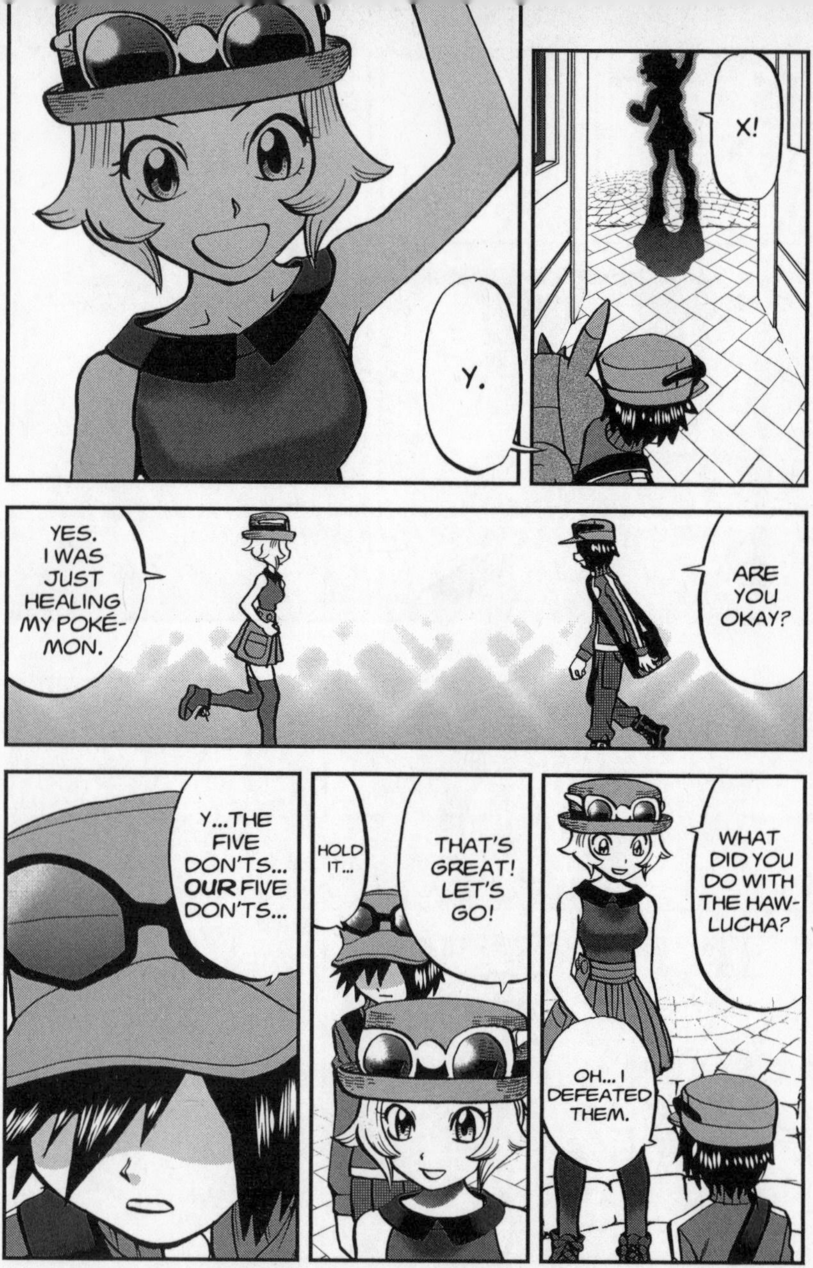
X!
Y.
ARE YOU OKAY?
YES. I WAS JUST HEALING MY POKÉ-MON.
WHAT DID YOU DO WITH THE HAW-LUCHA?
OH... I DEFEATED THEM.
THAT'S GREAT! LET'S GO!
HOLD IT...
Y...THE FIVE DON'TS... **OUR** FIVE DON'TS...

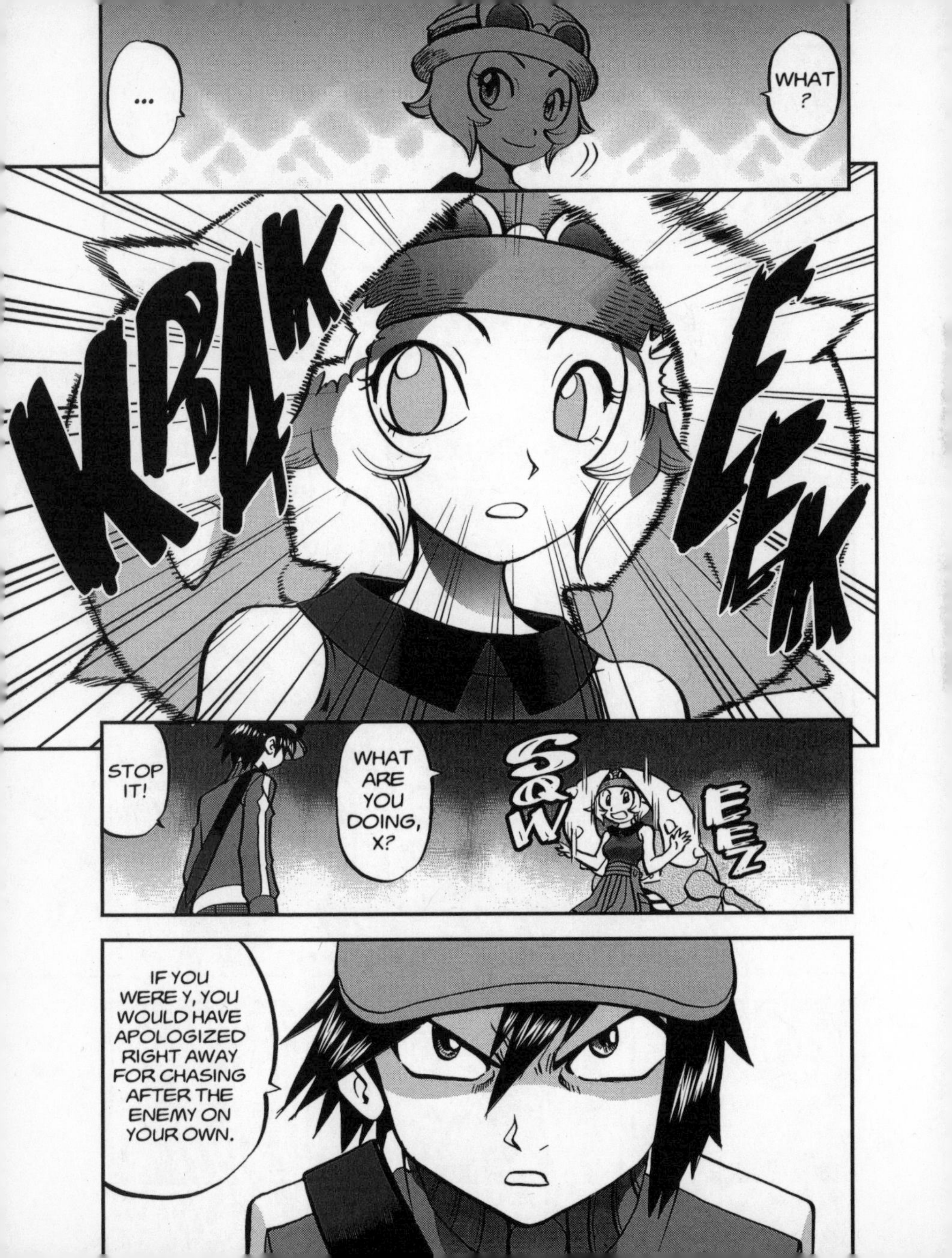
WHAT ?
...
SQW EEZ
WHAT ARE YOU DOING, X?
STOP IT!
IF YOU WERE Y, YOU WOULD HAVE APOLOGIZED RIGHT AWAY FOR CHASING AFTER THE ENEMY ON YOUR OWN.

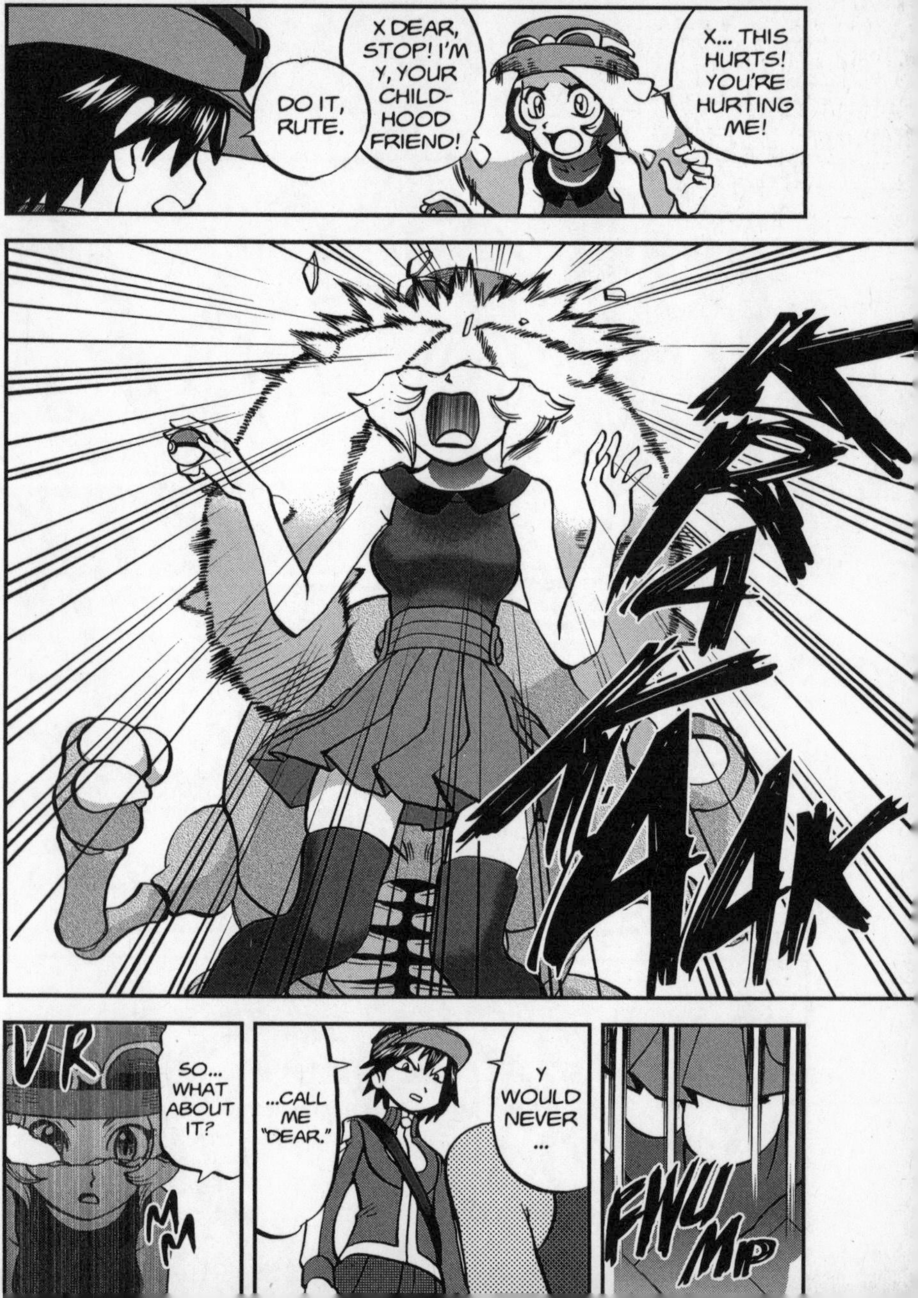
X... THIS HURTS! YOU'RE HURTING ME!
X DEAR, STOP! I'M Y, YOUR CHILDHOOD FRIEND!
DO IT, RUTE.
FWUMP
Y WOULD NEVER ...
...CALL ME "DEAR."
SO... WHAT ABOUT IT?
VR
MM

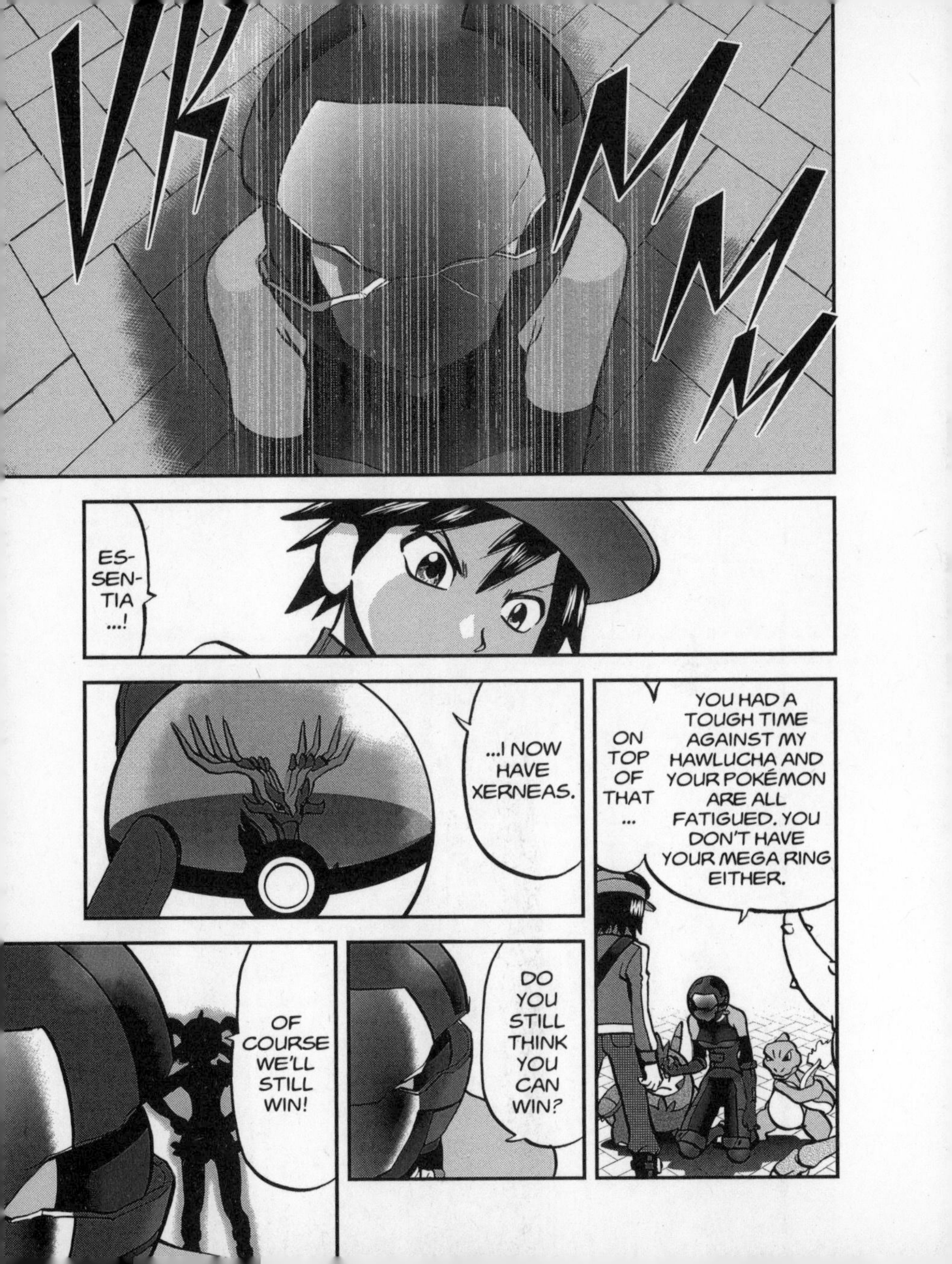
VKMMMM
ES-SEN-TIA...!
YOU HAD A TOUGH TIME AGAINST MY HAWLUCHA AND YOUR POKÉMON ARE ALL FATIGUED. YOU DON'T HAVE YOUR MEGA RING EITHER.
ON TOP OF THAT...
...I NOW HAVE XERNEAS.
DO YOU STILL THINK YOU CAN WIN?
OF COURSE WE'LL STILL WIN!

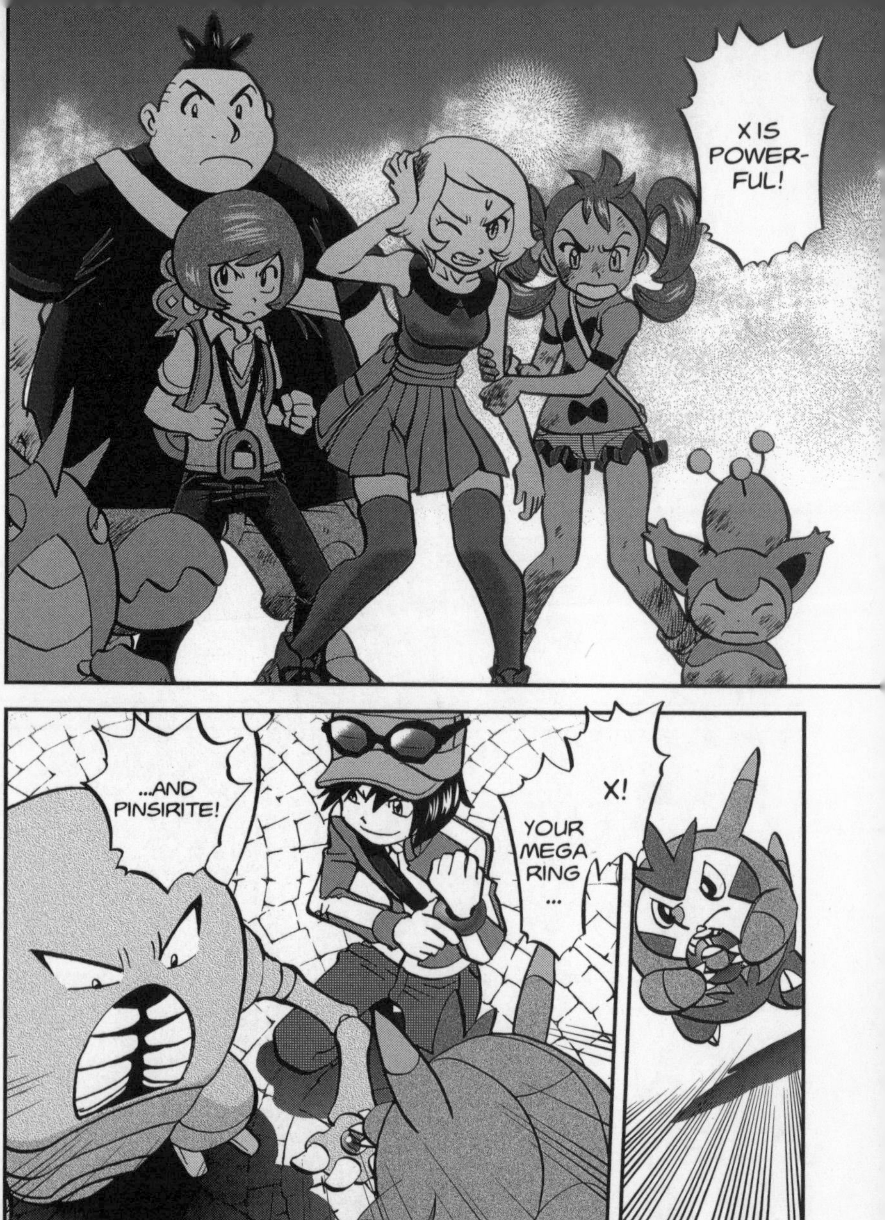
X IS POWER-FUL!
X!
YOUR MEGA RING ...
...AND PINSIRITE!

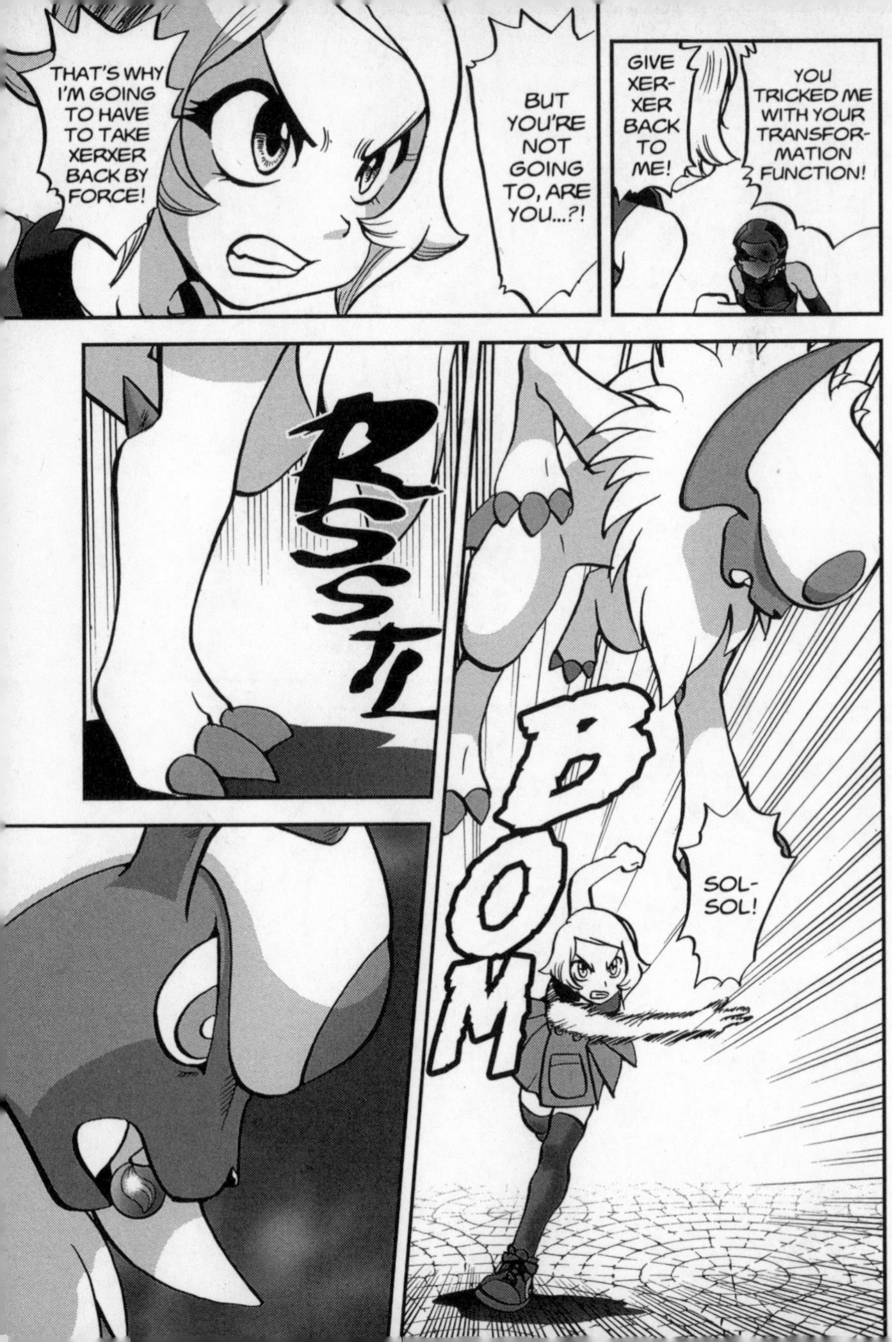
YOU TRICKED ME WITH YOUR TRANSFORMATION FUNCTION!
GIVE XERXER BACK TO ME!
BUT YOU'RE NOT GOING TO, ARE YOU...?!
THAT'S WHY I'M GOING TO HAVE TO TAKE XERXER BACK BY FORCE!
BOOM
SOL-SOL!
RSSTL

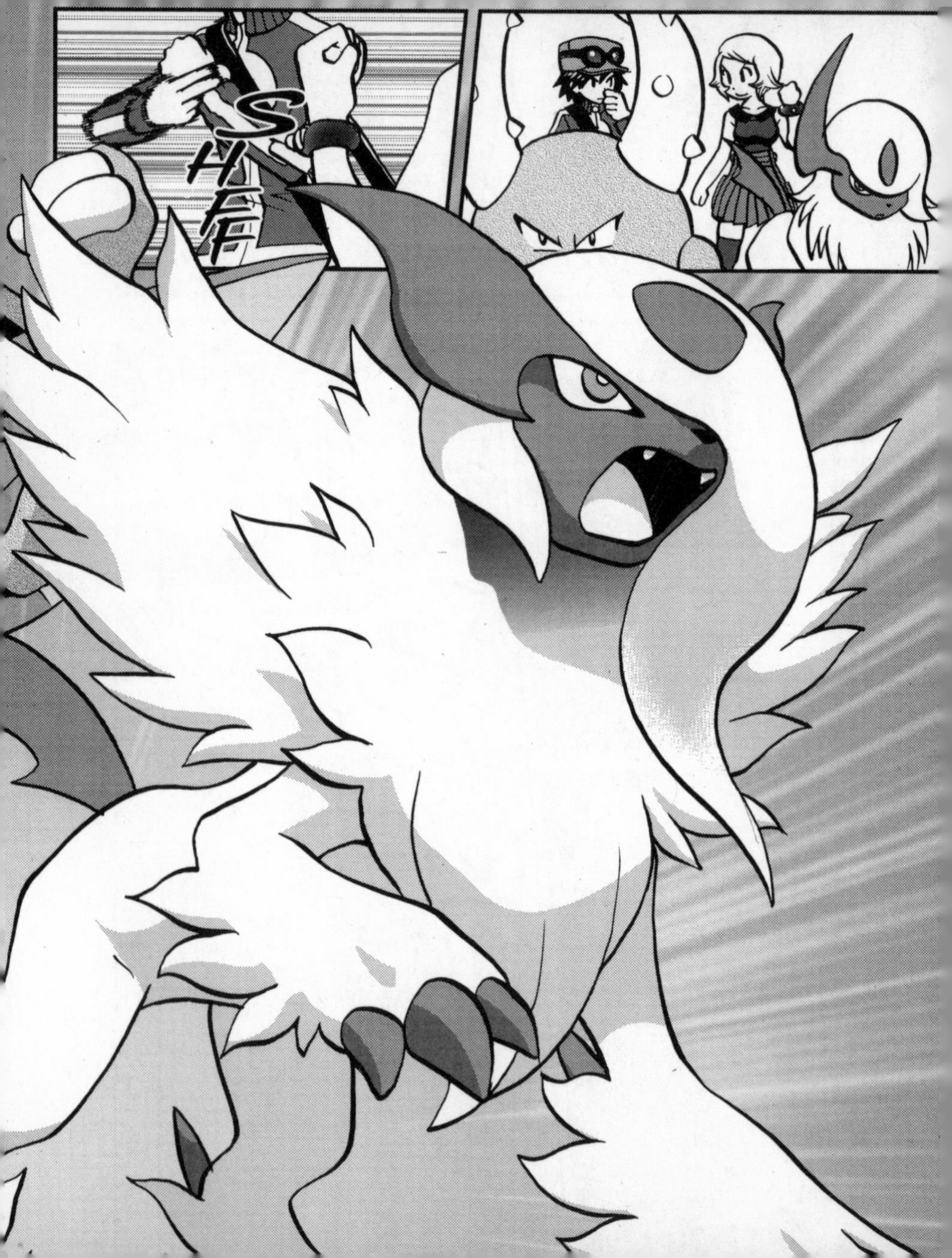
SHFF

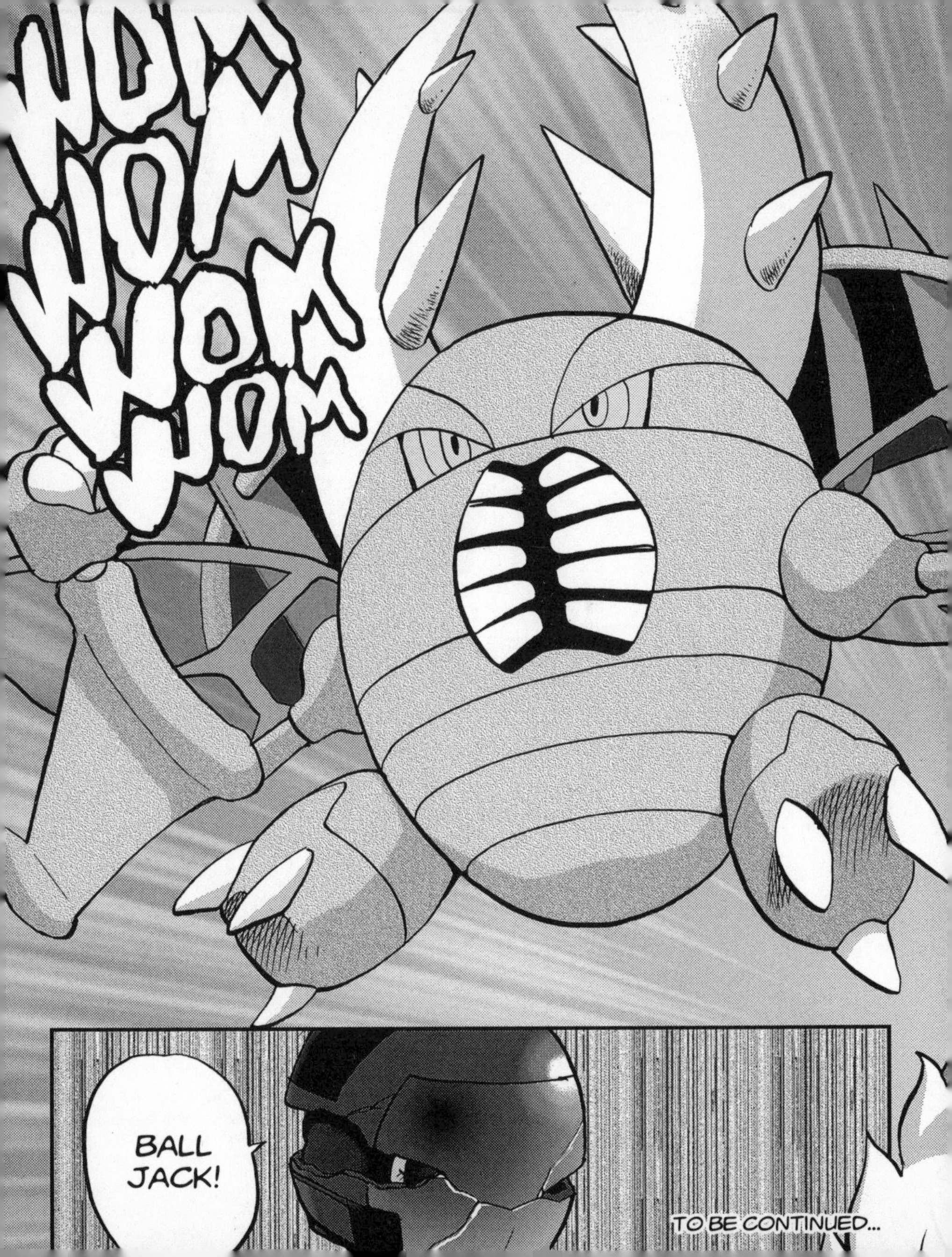
WOM WOM WOM WOM
BALL JACK!
TO BE CONTINUED...

Current Location

Anistar City

Some say the enigmatic device used
as a sundial came from outer space.

Pokémon X • Y
Volume 9
Perfect Square Edition

Story by HIDENORI KUSAKA
Art by SATOSHI YAMAMOTO

©2017 The Pokémon Company International.
©1995–2017 Nintendo / Creatures Inc. / GAME FREAK inc.
TM, ®, and character names are trademarks of Nintendo.
POCKET MONSTERS SPECIAL X•Y Vol. 5
by Hidenori KUSAKA, Satoshi YAMAMOTO
© 2014 Hidenori KUSAKA, Satoshi YAMAMOTO
All rights reserved.
Original Japanese edition published by SHOGAKUKAN.
English translation rights in the United States of America, Canada, the United Kingdom,
Ireland, Australia, New Zealand and India arranged with SHOGAKUKAN.

English Adaptation—Bryant Turnage
Translation—Tetsuichiro Miyaki
Touch-up & Lettering—Annaliese Christman
Design—Shawn Carrico
Editor—Annette Roman

Printed in the U.S.A.

Published by
VIZ Media, LLC
P.O. Box 77010
San Francisco, CA 94107

10 9 8 7 6 5 4 3
First printing, January 2017
Third printing, January 2018

PARENTAL ADVISORY
POKÉMON ADVENTURES
is rated A and is suitable
for readers of all ages.
ratings.viz.com

www.perfectsquare.com   www.viz.com

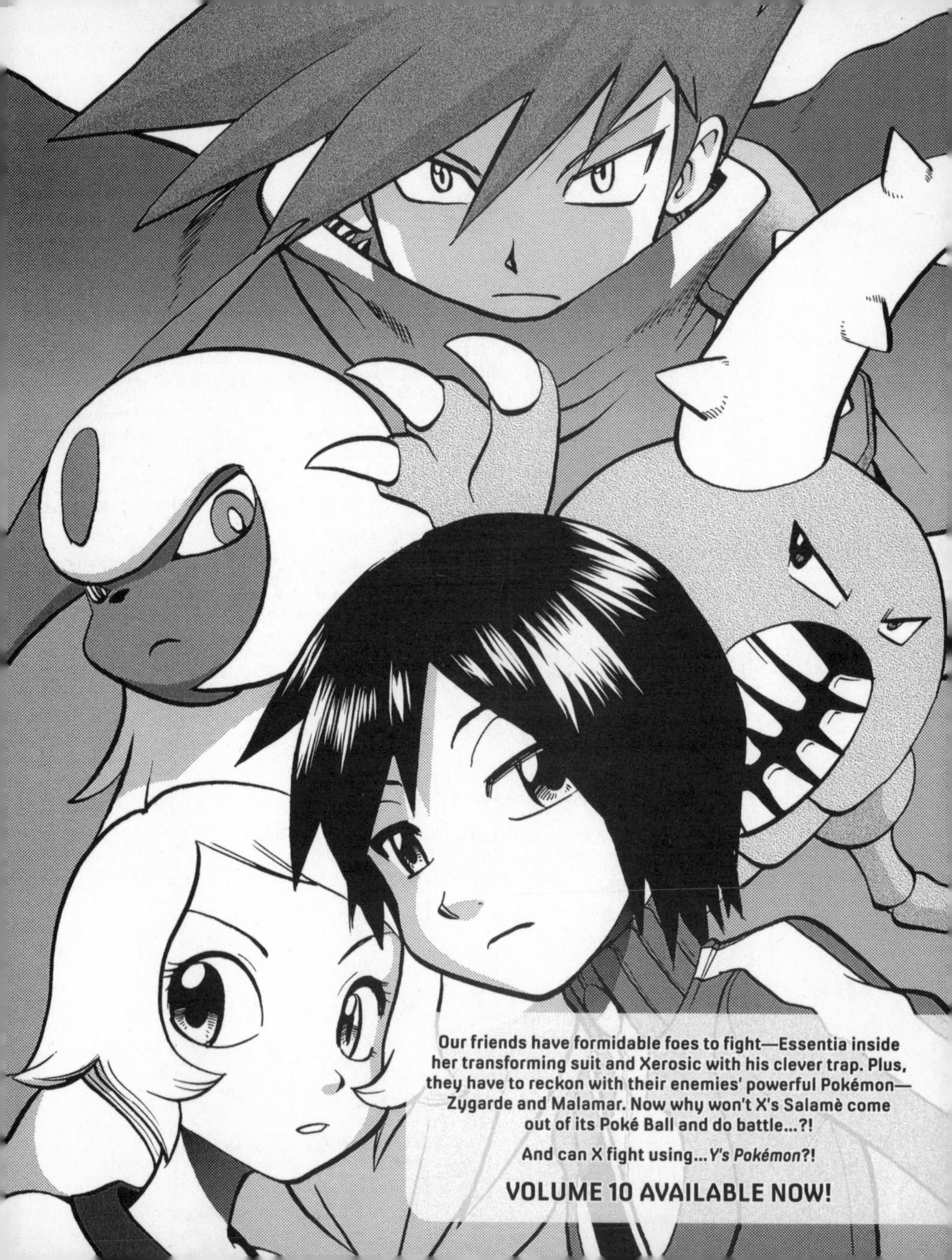
Our friends have formidable foes to fight—Essentia inside her transforming suit and Xerosic with his clever trap. Plus, they have to reckon with their enemies' powerful Pokémon—Zygarde and Malamar. Now why won't X's Salamè come out of its Poké Ball and do battle...?!
And can X fight using... *Y's Pokémon*?!
VOLUME 10 AVAILABLE NOW!

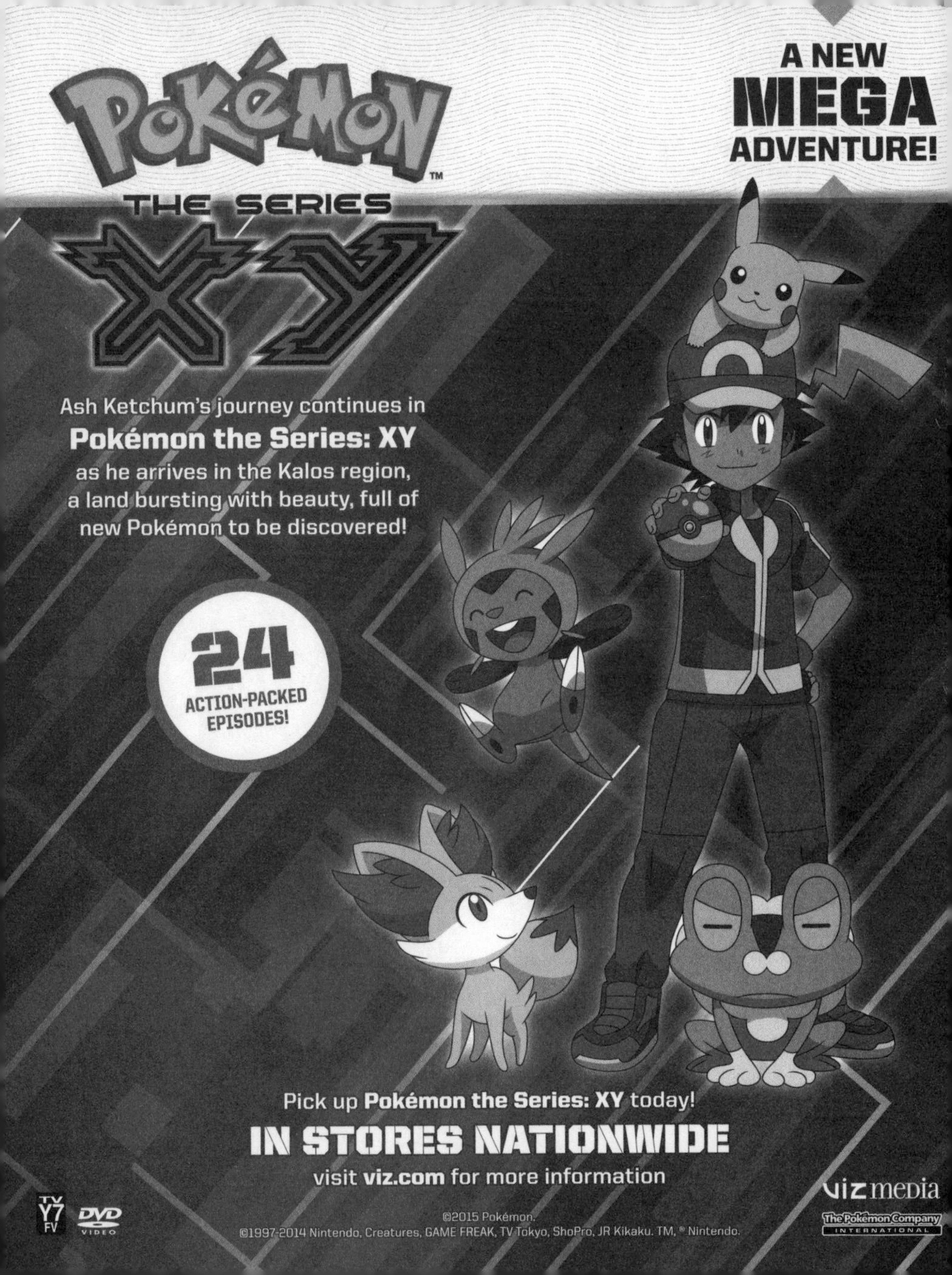
Pokémon™
THE SERIES
XY
A NEW
MEGA
ADVENTURE!
Ash Ketchum's journey continues in
Pokémon the Series: XY
as he arrives in the Kalos region,
a land bursting with beauty, full of
new Pokémon to be discovered!
24
ACTION-PACKED
EPISODES!
Pick up Pokémon the Series: XY today!
IN STORES NATIONWIDE
visit viz.com for more information
TV Y7 FV
DVD VIDEO
viz media
The Pokémon Company INTERNATIONAL
©2015 Pokémon.
©1997-2014 Nintendo, Creatures, GAME FREAK, TV Tokyo, ShoPro, JR Kikaku. TM, ® Nintendo.

POCKET COMICS

STORY & ART BY SANTA HARUKAZE

BLACK & WHITE

LEGENDARY POKÉMON

X•Y

A Pokémon pocket-sized book chock-full of four-panel gags, Pokémon trivia and fun quizzes based on the characters you know and love!

viz media

www.viz.com

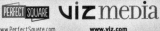

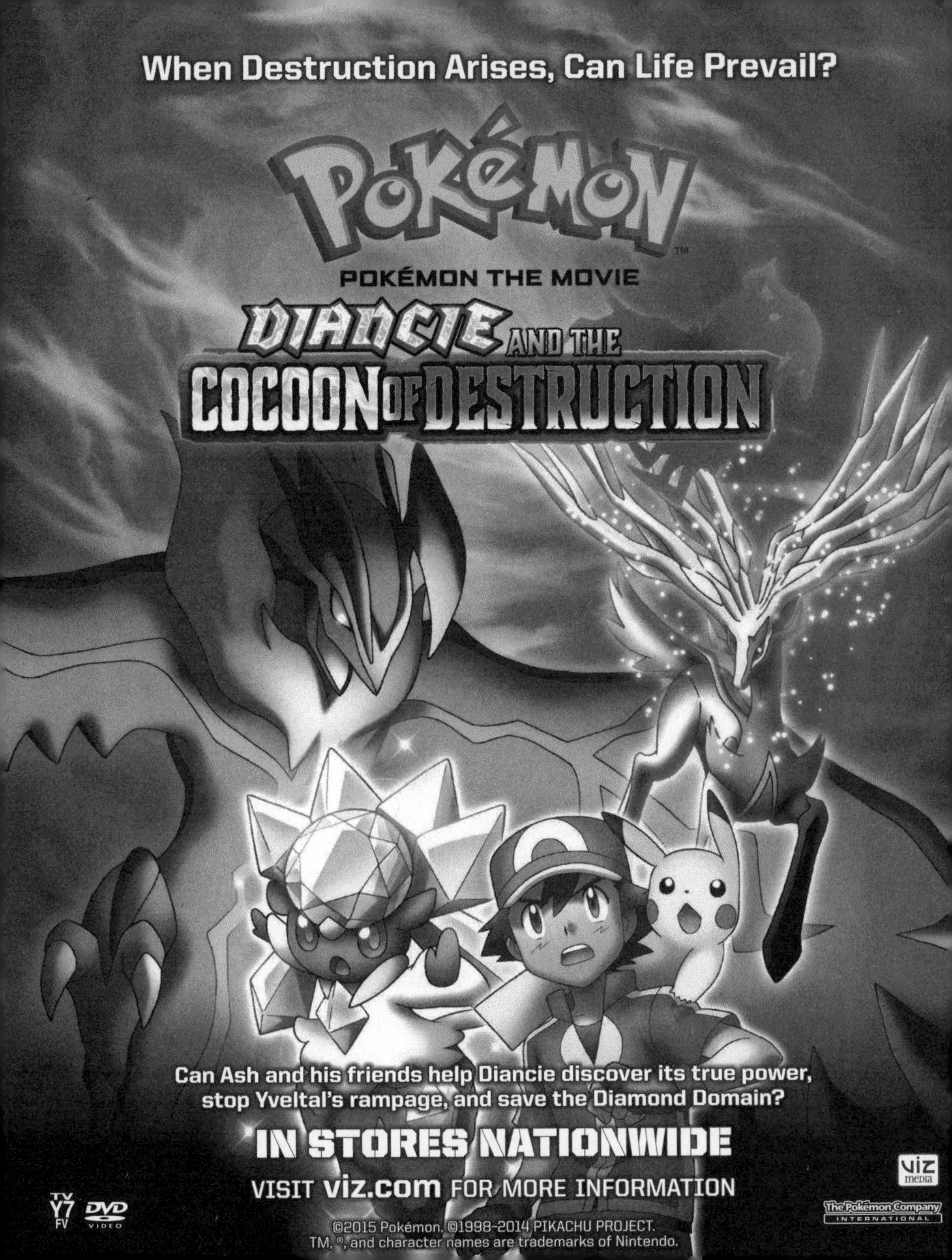
When Destruction Arises, Can Life Prevail?
POKÉMON
POKÉMON THE MOVIE
DIANCIE AND THE COCOON OF DESTRUCTION
Can Ash and his friends help Diancie discover its true power, stop Yveltal's rampage, and save the Diamond Domain?
IN STORES NATIONWIDE
VISIT viz.com FOR MORE INFORMATION
TV Y7 FV
DVD VIDEO
VIZ media
The Pokémon Company INTERNATIONAL
©2015 Pokémon. ©1998-2014 PIKACHU PROJECT.
TM, ®, and character names are trademarks of Nintendo.

The adventure continues in the Johto region!

POKÉMON™ ADVENTURES

GOLD & SILVER BOX SET

Includes POKÉMON ADVENTURES Vols. 8-14 and a collectible poster!

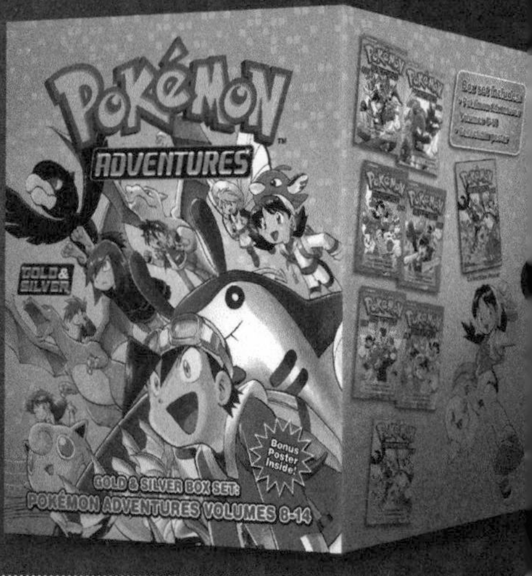

POKÉMON
ADVENTURES
GOLD & SILVER
Bonus Poster Inside!
GOLD & SILVER BOX SET:
POKÉMON ADVENTURES VOLUMES 8-14

Story by
HIDENORI KUSAKA

Art by
**MATO,
SATOSHI YAMAMOTO**

More exciting Pokémon adventures starring Gold and his rival Silver! First someone steals Gold's backpack full of Poké Balls (and Pokémon!). Then someone steals Prof. Elm's Totod Can Gold catch the thief—or thieves?!

Keep an eye on Team Rocket, Gold... Could they be behind this crime wave?

viz media
www.viz.com
PERFECT SQUARE